"Mike, there's... you now."

If that was going to happen, it was better that it happen now, she told herself, trying to get psyched up to tell Mike the truth.

"Kayla." He touched her hand, a split-second touch. It happened so fast, she wasn't sure if she'd really felt it or not. "Spit it out," he said.

"Okay." She took a deep breath and let it out again, slowly. "You know when we dated and then broke up?"

He nodded, his eyes intent on her.

"I told you there was a reason I wanted to find you when you blocked me."

"Yeah," he said. "I'm really sorry about that. It was rude and inexcusable."

"Well...yes. It was." Again, she sucked in a breath and let it out. "Mike, the reason I wanted to get in touch with you was...I found out I was pregnant."

His eyes went wide. "Did I hear that right? You got pregnant?"

She nodded, lifted her chin and straightened her shoulders. "You heard me right. Emma is your daughter."

Lee Tobin McClain is the *New York Times* bestselling author of emotional small-town romances featuring flawed characters who find healing through friendship, faith and family. Lee grew up in Ohio and now lives in Western Pennsylvania, where she enjoys hiking with her goofy goldendoodle, visiting writer friends and admiring her daughter's mastery of the latest TikTok dances. Learn more about her books at leetobinmcclain.com.

Books by Lee Tobin McClain

Love Inspired

Tumbleweed, Texas

The Coach's Secret Child

K-9 Companions

Her Easter Prayer
The Veteran's Holiday Home
A Friend to Trust
A Companion for Christmas
A Companion for His Son
His Christmas Salvation
The Veteran's Valentine Helper
Holding Onto Secrets
Her Surprise Neighbor
An Unexpected Christmas Helper

Rescue Haven

The Secret Christmas Child
Child on His Doorstep
Finding a Christmas Home

Visit the Author Profile page at LoveInspired.com for more titles.

THE COACH'S SECRET CHILD

LEE TOBIN McCLAIN

LOVE INSPIRED
INSPIRATIONAL ROMANCE

If you purchased this book without a cover you should be aware that this book is stolen property. It was reported as "unsold and destroyed" to the publisher, and neither the author nor the publisher has received any payment for this "stripped book."

Special thanks and acknowledgment are given to
Lee Tobin McClain for her contribution to the
Tumbleweed, Texas miniseries.

LOVE INSPIRED®
INSPIRATIONAL ROMANCE

ISBN-13: 978-1-335-23039-3

The Coach's Secret Child

Recycling programs for this product may not exist in your area

Copyright © 2026 by Harlequin Enterprises ULC

All rights reserved. No part of this book may be used or reproduced in any manner whatsoever without written permission.

Without limiting the exclusive rights of any author, contributor or the publisher of this publication, any unauthorized use of this publication to train generative artificial intelligence (AI) technologies is expressly prohibited. Harlequin also exercises their rights under Article 4(3) of the Digital Single Market Directive 2019/790 and expressly reserves this publication from the text and data mining exception.

This is a work of fiction. Names, characters, places and incidents are either the product of the author's imagination or are used fictitiously. Any resemblance to actual persons, living or dead, businesses, companies, events or locales is entirely coincidental.

For questions and comments about the quality of this book, please contact us at CustomerService@Harlequin.com.

® is a trademark of Harlequin Enterprises ULC.

Love Inspired	HarperCollins Publishers
22 Adelaide St. West, 41st Floor	Macken House, 39/40 Mayor Street Upper,
Toronto, Ontario M5H 4E3, Canada	Dublin 1, D01 C9W8, Ireland
www.LoveInspired.com	www.HarperCollins.com

Printed in U.S.A.

> Rejoice evermore. Pray without ceasing.
> In every thing give thanks: for this is the will of God
> in Christ Jesus concerning you.
> —*1 Thessalonians* 5:16–18

To my favorite former football player, Bill. Thank you for sharing your knowledge and love of the game.

Chapter One

Kayla Stewart walked into the Tumbleweed High media center and nabbed a seat at the end of the back row. Teachers' meetings could run long, and she had to pick up her two-year-old daughter by five o'clock.

Principal Ron Garcia strode down the aisle and stopped beside her. "Favor to ask you," he said.

"Sure, whatever you need." Principal Garcia had done Kayla a real service this year, scheduling her planning period for the beginning of the day so that she could come in a little later. It was super helpful as she navigated her daughter's first year in day care. She owed him big-time. And she really, really wanted to keep the same schedule for next year.

Of course, her father had tried to pay for a nanny. But she needed her independence, and she needed to model hard work and female strength for the daughter who was everything to her.

"Could you mentor the new history teacher?" the principal asked. "He'll be in the classroom next door to you, and you share a lot of students, so it'll be convenient."

Relieved that the favor wasn't too time-consuming, Kayla smiled. "Of course. I'm glad you finally found someone." Since the previous teacher had gone on medical leave, a variety of short-term subs had filled the role. It would be good for the students to have more consistency.

"Yes, we're pleased." His expression was cryptic. "Thank you for agreeing to help. He's one of three new teachers I'll be introducing today."

As the meeting got started with announcements and schedule changes, Kayla's best friend on the faculty, Ariella Jackson, slid into the seat next to her. "What did I miss?" she whispered.

"Nothing you haven't heard a million times before." While Kayla was only a second-year teacher, Ariella had been at it for almost twenty years. In fact, she'd served as Kayla's mentor when she'd first started.

Around them, teachers shuffled papers and surreptitiously checked their phones. It was an unusually warm day for February, even in East

Texas. The windows were open, but the fresh, springlike air wasn't enough to disguise the faint odor of sweaty teenagers.

Everyone, including Kayla, was eager to escape. The business of the meeting dragged on, but finally, Principal Garcia started introducing the new teachers and asking them to say a few words. One, a math teacher, had been there since the beginning of January but was still excited about coming on board officially. The next, a chemistry teacher, had a been-there-done-that attitude.

"And now," Principal Garcia said, "I'd like to introduce our third new hire, history teacher and our new head football coach, Mr. Cook!"

Kayla let her head drop back and stared at the ceiling, letting out a sigh. She had to mentor the coach? She was the least sports-oriented person in their football-obsessed town of Tumbleweed, Texas.

"Mike's being mentored by Kayla Stewart," the principal said. "Mike, come on up and tell us a little about yourself."

Wait a minute. His name was Mike Cook? It couldn't be...

No, she reassured herself as her heart rate sped up. It was a common name.

A very tall, very brawny man with short

brown hair trotted up the steps and strode to the podium.

Oh... Kayla out a sigh, feeling her insides turn to jelly. She remembered how comforting those muscular arms had felt, holding her. She remembered that strong, square jaw and the smile that had seemed like it was for her alone.

She remembered the sober expression on his face when he'd told her it wasn't going to work between them after all. How she'd cried and begged him to reconsider. And then...

No. She wouldn't let those memories flood her brain and her heart. She tuned back in to her surroundings and the excited whispers around her.

"He is *hot*," said a teacher in front of her.

"Totally hot," another murmured in response.

"Single, do you think?"

"I heard he played in the NFL!"

"Wonder if he has a clue about teaching?"

Up in the front of the room, Mike had started to speak. "As a new teacher, I'm here to learn," he said. "I want to do my best by these kids academically. That's the priority."

"But we want to win football games," a teacher near the front called out in a fake-whiny voice, and there was good-natured laughter.

"That's the second priority," Mike said with

that devastating, dimpled smile that had melted Kayla's heart three years ago.

Female sighs sounded all around her. Obviously, she wasn't the only one to be affected by Mike's good looks and friendly, self-assured demeanor.

"My third priority is to find a place to live that's not the motel, so if anyone knows of a rental..."

"You can stay at my place, honey," called a brash older teacher, causing general laughter.

Mike's smile slipped a little. He looked away and rubbed the back of his neck.

"Is he blushing?" Ariella asked in a low voice.

"Aw, he's shy," someone else said.

Shy? Mike?

"Okay, okay," Principal Garcia said. "Thank you, Mike. Everyone, remember that our spring parent-teacher night is next Thursday. Mentors, please stay long enough to set up a formal meeting with your mentees. Everyone else, get outa here."

Kayla took deep, calming breaths as her colleagues gathered their things.

Of all the high schools in the state of Texas, why on earth had Mike Cook landed in hers?

In weak moments, late at night, she'd looked him up online. She'd learned of his career-ending injury and had read an interview where he'd said he intended to make use of his education degree and go back into teaching.

Then he'd dropped out of sight. Never in a million years had she expected he'd end up here. And what were the odds that she'd be chosen to be his teaching mentor?

"Have fun," Ariella said, patting her shoulder and then joining the herd rushing out the door.

Kayla closed her eyes and silently prayed for help. Then she swallowed hard and pushed herself out of her chair. Her knees felt wobbly, her face hot.

What kind of man had Mike become in the past three years? Was he still as unpredictable as he'd been before, warm and loving one minute, cold the next?

How was his character—the thing she hadn't considered when she'd fallen for him?

And most pressing: Should she tell this man she'd never expected to see again that he was the father of her child?

As Mike Cook greeted faculty and staff members who'd stayed to say hello, his mind raced.

His new faculty mentor was Kayla Stewart.

At first, he hadn't believed it could be the

same woman he'd known before. What were the odds? Yes, she'd said she'd studied education, but to his knowledge, she hadn't been using her teaching degree back then. He'd figured she was still living the bohemian life in Austin. That was how he'd pictured her, which he tended to do way too often.

He couldn't deny that he was curious and eager to see her again. Three years, and he'd never forgotten her.

But overriding the eagerness was shame at how he'd ended the relationship. He'd hurt her badly. He hadn't had a choice, and she was better off, but he'd done a lot wrong in their short time together and he regretted it deeply.

There was no question of making it up to her, nor of reconnecting on an emotional level. That way lay disaster, given who he was and where he came from. So the question was, would they be able to work together, or did they need to end this mentoring relationship before it began?

Maybe she'd changed enough that she wouldn't find him appealing, or would hold no appeal for him. Maybe she'd married, although if that was the case, she hadn't taken her husband's last name.

As the room cleared, the peripheral vision that had made him a strong receiver in the NFL revealed a woman approaching. He turned, and his mouth went dry.

It was Kayla.

She looked different, all right. More mature. Professional. Less cute, more beautiful.

Definitely still way too appealing.

Had she known she'd be mentoring him? Asked to do it, even? Would that be good or bad?

She approached and stood in front of him, arms crossed. "I wasn't expecting you," she said without smiling. "Principal Garcia just sprung this on me before the meeting today."

Well, that answers that question.

"I didn't know you'd be here, either." He paused and glanced around to ensure they wouldn't be overheard. "Are you able to work with me? As a new teacher, I can't rock the boat, but you could ask."

She tilted her head to one side. "Are you kidding? You're the head football coach. You have more status than any other teacher in the school."

She sounded bitter. Understandable. "I can ask for a change."

"No," she said. "It's fine. I can be professional in the interest of staying on Principal Garcia's good side."

That sounded completely unlike the carefree, creative person she'd been. "Are you sure? It's a big school. I'm sure there are other mentors he could tap."

"No." She was shaking her head. Her hair, which had been long and wavy when he'd known her before, now swung neatly at shoulder length. Still shiny, though. Probably just as soft as it had been when...

He pulled himself back into the present and reached for a businesslike tone. "When can you meet? Is now good?"

"No. I have to pick up my daughter at day care."

She had a daughter? He felt his eyebrows shoot up. "I didn't know you'd gotten married."

"I'm not anymore."

Wow, she was not the innocent, sweet girl he'd known.

And you had a lot to do with that, his conscience reminded him.

"I can meet tomorrow or Thursday after school," she said, her voice impatient. "My dad can pick up Emma from day care."

"Emma." He couldn't help smiling, because he liked the name. "How old is she?"

Her face tightened. "She's two. Almost three."

So, Kayla had gotten involved with someone

else shortly after he'd ended things with her. Had it been a rebound thing, or totally unrelated to him?

The media center was empty now, save for a custodian emptying trash cans. The carpet was worn, and the books on the shelves that lined the room looked old. The place could definitely use a facelift, and more.

He'd already seen the football field and stadium during his interview. Both were new looking and immaculate. That showed the town's priorities. But he'd meant it when he'd said that academics were the most important thing for young people. He knew all too well that sports were not the be-all and end-all. Even star athletes needed a backup plan.

He was a prime example of that, himself.

Kayla pulled out her phone and checked the time. "I need to get going."

"How about tomorrow after school? We could get dinner."

"No." She lifted her chin. "I'd rather meet here at the school."

Something made him want to push her. "You have to eat," he said. "We both do. How about an early dinner at the Friendly Fork Diner?"

She took a step back and propped a hand on her hip. He remembered that stance from when they'd been together. It had been cute then, and it was still cute.

Her words weren't. "Look, this isn't going to be a friendly kind of thing. It's strictly professional. Let's meet in my classroom, right after school."

"Fine," he said.

She spun and walked away. As he watched her, he sighed.

This wasn't going to be easy.

Chapter Two

By the end of the school day on Wednesday, Kayla was exhausted. She longed to just pick up Emma and go home.

Instead, she had to meet with the man who'd fathered her child and broken her heart.

She straightened desks the kids had moved around while working in groups, and picked up a couple of pencils, a phone case, and a tube of lip gloss from the floor. Then she went to the whiteboard and erased the day's motto and lesson plan, moving slowly.

She'd barely slept last night, worrying about how things would go with Mike. He could refuse to acknowledge Emma. He could get angry that she hadn't found him and let him know he was a father, that she hadn't tried hard enough.

He could turn out to be a bad guy, not suitable to play a role in Emma's life.

That was her biggest fear, and that was what she wanted to figure out, starting with this meeting. Was he worthy of being a father to Emma? Was he even good with kids? Did he have a dangerous or violent streak? Would he dump Emma when he lost interest, just like he'd dumped Kayla?

They really hadn't known each other well when they'd jumped into their three-month long relationship. At twenty-five, enjoying her freedom and anonymity in Austin, she hadn't felt the details were important. She didn't know exactly where he'd grown up, nor who his parents were, because he'd been vague about it when they'd known each other. She hadn't minded; she'd been vague about her own background, too, not wanting to let anyone know that she was from one of the wealthier families in Southeast Texas.

Now that Emma's safety and happiness were involved, vagueness wasn't an option. She needed to know more about him, both what he said and what he left unsaid.

There was a tap on the doorframe of her classroom. "Is now still good?" Mike asked.

He wore a white dress shirt with rolled-up sleeves, dark slacks, and high-end leather sneakers. Perfectly conservative and appropriate, and yet he managed to look like a hot male model. That short, dark hair, those brawny forearms, that bit of beard stubble…

He came in a few steps, smiling his killer smile. "Do you want to meet now? In here or my classroom?"

"It's fine," she snapped, annoyed at her own reaction to him. "I don't have much time. And I'd rather meet in the teachers' lounge."

"Sure, okay. But first…" He closed the classroom door behind him. "Look, I wanted to tell you I'm sorry for how things ended. Before. I just…there were reasons I needed to make a change, but I went about it in all the wrong ways and I apologize for that."

That was the most non-apology apology she'd ever heard. No explanation and precious little sincerity. Well, two could play that game. She lifted her chin. "There were reasons I needed to talk with you after things ended, instead of being completely shut out. But it's water under the bridge at this point. Don't worry about it."

He studied her, his head tilted to one side. "You sure you can work with me?"

"Yes. Come on. Let's walk and talk." She grabbed her laptop and coffee cup and led the way out of the classroom.

The hallway was nearly empty, with just a few students talking beside their lockers. Laughter came from a classroom where two teachers stood. The typical smells mingled: disinfectant, fried meat from the tacos served at lunchtime in the cafeteria, and sweat.

Kayla sipped her coffee and made a face. Cold and stale.

A couple of female teachers walked past them with smiles and greetings. Then two bigger boys, whom Kayla knew slightly, emerged from the gym. "Hey, Coach," one said, and then both nodded politely at her. "Hey, Miss Stewart."

"Weight training tomorrow before school, guys," Mike called back over his shoulder. Then he looked at Kayla. "Who are they?"

"Jose and Ricky Huerta. Twins. Good kids. Have you met with the team yet?"

"We had a meet and greet after school on Monday. Poorly attended. Tomorrow, we start optional workouts, but I'm not sure anyone will show up."

"You may have an uphill battle," she said as they arrived at the teachers' lounge. She reached for the door, but he stepped around her and opened it, holding it for her. "Thanks. The team has been on a losing streak, as I'm sure you know."

"I'm aware." He followed her to a small round table beside the soda machines. The lounge was empty except for a pair of math teachers leaning over a laptop, and Mindy Prescott, the art teacher, who paced back and forth talking on her phone.

They sat down, and Kayla got right to business. "How has this week gone so far, in the classroom?"

He shook his head. "Not as well as I like. The kids don't listen. They get up and walk out. They're on their phones."

"Hmm. They know better. Wonder why they're testing you so early?" She frowned. "Maybe it's because they've had a succession of subs before you."

"I started out being very clear about the rules," he said. "Posted them all around the classroom and went over them with the kids."

Kayla would have started with some community-building icebreakers, but she knew that wasn't everyone's style. "Did you get input from the kids about the rules?"

He blew out a puff of air. "I'm not really a fan of that strategy, though I did hear about it in my ed classes. I didn't use it in my student teaching, and it worked fine."

She shrugged. "Different district. You were in Austin to student teach?"

"Yes, a suburb."

"Our rural kids are unique," she said. "So,

you said you made the rules. Were they enforceable?"

He winced. "No, and I should have known better than to make a promise I couldn't keep."

"Seems to be your..." She trailed off. No need to bring up the past. "What happened?"

He narrowed his eyes, but didn't follow up on her implied words. "If someone walks out, I can't go after them. I have the rest of the students to teach. And if I tell someone to leave, if they've done something ridiculous...sometimes, they just don't go. I don't know all their names yet, so half the time, I don't know who to call out for problem behavior."

"That one's easy to fix." She opened her laptop to the school's learning management system and showed him how to pull up each class's roster, along with a photo of the student. "And if someone won't leave, you can call security to remove them."

He shook his head. "I hate to do that. I'm twice the size of the security guard, at least the one I met."

He was twice the size of most people. "Yeah, but like you pointed out, you have other students to teach. You can't be getting into a brawl with a student."

He sat back in his chair and blew out a breath.

"I have a lot to learn. It's not like I graduated from high school all that long ago, but kids are different now. We respected authority figures, at least to their faces."

"Yeah, that's not so much the case now," she said. "Or, let me correct that. A lot of the kids here are good and respectful. There are a few, though, that have an attitude toward teachers. Toward any staffers. We have to figure out different ways to manage them."

"I'll work on it." He sounded discouraged.

"It's a process," she said. "You'll learn."

They leaned over the computer again and she showed him where to post grades and homework assignments in the school's online system. They were close enough that she could feel the heat from his leg and his brawny arm.

Vicki Berlin, one of the math teachers who'd been working across the room, teetered over in her trademark three-inch heels. "How's it going, honey?" she asked, propping her hands on the table and leaning toward them.

"I'm still learning the ropes." Mike smiled nervously at her and then looked back at Kayla. "Making some mistakes."

"First year's the hardest," Kayla reassured him. "Isn't that the truth, Vicki?"

"Absolutely. You two take care." She walked away and left the lounge.

When Kayla looked around, she realized that the room was empty. Great. She was alone with Mike. Just what she'd been trying to avoid when she'd suggested meeting in the teachers' lounge.

"If there's nothing else, let's get going. It seems like you're doing fine." It was true. She hadn't seen any red flags in Mike. He'd listened attentively to her, admitted his mistakes, and seemed to be taking teaching seriously.

He seemed like he might be okay to know Emma, to play a role in her life. But he was risky in another way: dangerous to her heart.

She was still having that same visceral reaction to him as the moment they'd first met. Now, though, she'd gained enough life experience to know she needed to stay far away from that type of man. From any man, at this point. She was raising her daughter to be independent, and she meant to model that quality.

Besides, men like Mike—and men like her late husband, Beau, for that matter—didn't stick around. They weren't trustworthy, at least not as romantic partners. They were a risk she wasn't willing to take, not for herself and not for her daughter.

Which meant she needed to keep things purely professional where Mike was concerned.

As Mike left his motel room the next morning and drove to school, he couldn't get that meeting with Kayla Stewart out of his mind.

She'd been perfectly professional, and actually very helpful. But he could see that there was something simmering beneath the surface. No doubt it had to do with his own poor behavior toward her when he'd ended their brief relationship.

He'd done what he'd had to do. After getting so hurt and angry when he'd seen her with another guy—a guy who turned out to be just a friend—he'd realized he couldn't handle being in a relationship with a woman who evoked that much feeling in him.

He'd been cowardly to ghost her. But when he'd told her it was over, she'd cried, and it had taken every bit of his strength to stick to his plan and end things. He'd had to make it a hard break or he'd have had her right back in his arms, and he wouldn't have ever wanted to let her go.

The trouble was, she still evoked all kinds of feelings in him. She drew him like a porch light drew a moth.

He still wanted a relationship, wanted a wife actually, now that he'd become a Christian and realized that casual connections weren't the right way to be.

But not a wife like Kayla, who brought out a lot of strong, messy feelings. No, he wanted someone nice and calm, a good influence on him.

He had no choice but to work with Kayla, but he intended to limit their connection to work. He'd be strictly business with her, just as she seemed to intend to be strictly business with him. There was no need for her to know all the emotions she brought out in him. He intended to bury them deep inside.

When Mike reached the school at 6:25 a.m., he was basically holding his breath. Would anyone come to the team training session before classes?

There were cars in the parking lot, but those were likely to belong to the teachers. Many of them got to school very early.

The student parking lot looked empty. But he knew that most of the kids didn't have cars and either rode a bus or got dropped off by family members. He hoped that would be the case for his players, hoped that there would be a gang of them waiting to work out.

He headed straight for the weight room, his heart pounding with anticipation for the first workout he'd have with his new team.

The lights were on, but the room was empty.

Or not quite empty. There was Kayla, sitting on a bench at the side of the room, her head bent over a laptop.

He walked over to her. "What are you doing here?" he asked.

"Just being a good mentor," she said. "I thought I'd observe you interacting with the kids in a nonacademic setting first, but..." She looked around.

"But there are no kids," he said flatly.

He sat down beside her, a sweet, flowery scent from her slightly damp hair wafting in the air. Keep your distance, Cook, he reminded himself. Keep it professional.

He let his head sink into his hands. "What am I doing wrong?"

"Well, making the workout optional and at 6:30 a.m. might be the issue," she said. "Maybe after-school workouts would draw more of them in?"

"Good point," he said.

Just then, the door opened, and three sleepy-looking kids drifted in, then another. They wore a mix of workout gear, some of it high-end, some of it looking like it had been purchased at a discount store many years ago. That was typical of most high schools. Sports were a good equalizer, but to make that work, you had to help the less affluent kids with clothing and gear. He'd been on the receiving end of hand-me-down workout clothes himself, back at his rural high school a hundred miles to the west of Tumbleweed.

He hustled over to them, thanked them for coming, and got them warming up on the treadmills and stationary bikes. As he was talking, a few more kids meandered in.

He walked around, matching faces with the names he'd studied, encouraging them to get the blood flowing. After a few minutes, he got them going on a basic circuit workout, demonstrating the moves himself and sticking close to correct their form or to spot those lifting heavier weights.

The whole time, he was conscious that Kayla was there, watching him. He tried not to think about that and to focus on the kids instead.

Then he noticed a couple of boys looking over toward Kayla and laughing.

"Hey, show some respect," he said. He stepped between them Kayla, blocking their line of sight, and glared at the boys.

"Sorry, Coach," one of the kids said.

Mike understood how teen boys often acted, but he wouldn't permit any disrespect toward other teachers or toward women.

Definitely not toward Kayla.

Once he could see that everyone understood the workout, he stepped back and let them continue. He was watching for good form, strength, and work ethic. The positions for the fall season hadn't been assigned, of course, but he knew that certain kids were accustomed to playing certain roles. He wanted to make sure those positions were the right ones for these kids.

The boys laughed and argued and trash-talked as they woke up and became more alert. A couple more kids drifted into the room. It seemed there were two distinct groups: The kids from wealthier families, with brand-name workout clothes, and the rougher-edged kids who wore old T-shirts and sweats. A few members of each group seemed at odds with the others. He'd keep an eye on that, but didn't want to come down hard on them or make them feel like they couldn't talk freely during an offseason workout. He walked across the gym to where Kayla was sitting.

"What's the economic situation of the kids

here?" he asked her. "Seems varied. Do the differences cause problems?"

She looked at the kids for a moment. "You're right, there's a lot of economic diversity in our community," she said. "Sometimes the richer kids get into it with the poor ones."

Mike remembered that dynamic all too well. "Is it rural versus town kids?" he asked.

"Somewhat," she said, "but some of the ranch kids are quite well-off."

Mike was much more experienced with the poor kids, having been one himself, and he felt protective of them. However, he also didn't want to prejudge anyone. Poorer kids could have a chip on their shoulders. He certainly had.

"You just need to get to know them on an individual basis, and it'll become pretty clear who is struggling and who is, well, entitled." She wasn't looking at him as she spoke. She was watching the kids. "Uh-oh," she said. "That's Tyrell Love coming in. He and Winston Compton hate each other."

Mike could see immediately what she meant, reading the kids' body language. He left Kayla and walked back over to stand near the boys.

The voices in the weight room were getting louder as the kids got more comfortable and more alert.

A slight shoving match erupted where Winston and Tyrell were standing. When Mike approached, both boys turned away and focused on their workouts, but with a lot of under-the-breath muttering.

"We're a team," Mike reminded them. "If you're mad about something, take it out on the weights and on the field, not on each other."

The workout went on, mostly well, although he would've liked to have double the number of players attending. That was something to work on for next time.

From the corner of his eye, he saw Winston go up to another one of the poor kids, a scrawny guy who looked like he would be more suited to the physics team than to football. Winston shoved and bumped him.

"Compton," Mike called. "Get over here."

Winston glanced up, looked at the other students who had their eyes on him, and slowly walked over to Mike, making it clear that he wasn't jumping to anybody's command.

"I'm catching an attitude from you," Mike said. "You're used to playing quarterback, right? If you're the quarterback, I expect you to act like a leader."

Winston kicked a weight bench, then stomped out of the room.

Great. There goes our star. "Back to work, boys," he said to the others. "Ten minutes, and then you can clean up before classes start."

He glanced over at Kayla. She was watching, her expression concerned.

He'd never thought this job was going to be easy, but he thought he might have some skill at it. Now, he was having doubts.

It looked like Kayla was having doubts, too.

Chapter Three

On Thursday evening, Kayla helped Emma climb into her booster chair and kissed the top of her head. She poured milk for her daughter and glasses of iced tea for her father and herself. Then she scooped chili from the Crock-Pot into three bowls and carried them to the table.

"I'm glad you could stay for supper, Dad," she said.

"Always glad to eat with my two favorite girls."

Kayla laughed. She was far from the favorite. More like the black sheep of the family. But giving Dad a granddaughter, even under less-than-ideal circumstances, had made up for a lot of Kayla's youthful transgressions for a Texas girl from a wealthy family.

Plus, she'd returned to Tumbleweed while her brother was living in New York City and her sister was in LA. That counted for a lot with Dad.

Kayla sat down at the table, and they all held

hands for a prayer. As the sunset cast golden light into her little kitchen, Kayla consciously tried to relax her shoulders. "What did you and Gampy do today?" she asked Emma.

Emma's little fingers tapped on the worn wooden table, and she gave her grandfather a winning smile. "Got coff-fee," she said.

Kayla arched an eyebrow at her father and passed around shredded cheese and sour cream. "Did you drink coffee?" she asked Emma.

"Yes!" Emma cackled with delight.

Dad put a finger in front of his lips. "Emma, remember, that's our secret."

"Dad!" Kayla rolled her eyes. "You're such a bad influence."

"I gave her one sip, mostly milk and sugar," he said. "Got to get this little lady off to the right start."

Kayla shook her head as she started to eat, but she wasn't really upset. She looked at her father, his full head of white hair curling down his neck, his blue cotton shirt with rolled-up sleeves, his ruddy, weathered face. He was still a handsome man, but she didn't like the bags under his eyes. She knew he didn't sleep well, hadn't since Mom had died.

"Thanks so much for taking care of her today, Dad," Kayla said. The day care had had a waterline break and closed unexpectedly, and she was thankful Dad could step in at the last minute. That kind of family support was one reason she'd decided, shortly after learning she was pregnant, that she needed to move back to Tumbleweed, sacrificing some of her independence but gaining much-needed help. In addition to Dad, she had aunts and uncles and cousins in the area, and she valued the family network for herself as well as for Emma.

"How was your before-school meeting with the new coach?" Dad asked.

Kayla suppressed a sigh. Of course, Dad knew about that. As the former mayor of Tumbleweed, he knew almost everything that went on.

It worried her, though. It added to her concerns about the possibility of Mike being in Emma's life.

Dad would not be happy to find out that it was Mike who had broken the heart of his precious youngest daughter. And yet, if Mike learned the truth, Dad would find out. Just like he found out everything else about her life.

Each day has troubles enough of its own, she reminded herself. She'd worry about her father's reaction later. Now, she was just puzzling over whether Mike would be a good person to include in Emma's life.

If he even wanted to be included, which was an open question.

He seemed like a decent person. From what she could see, today had gone better for him in the classroom. There was less noise and disruption, and the couple of times she had glanced in, he seemed to be focused on teaching, with the kids paying attention.

Still, she was reserving judgment. Mike had, after all, broken up with her and blocked her on his phone. She wasn't going to let him do the same to her sweet child.

Her face covered with spots of red chili, Emma reached across the table toward the stack of corn bread pieces. Kayla helped her daughter to one. The corn bread was from a mix, which her mother would have disapproved of. But as a working mom, Kayla only had so much time on her hands.

"Well? What about that meeting?" Dad was waiting for her response.

"It was fine. I think Coach Mike is going to do well as a teacher."

"The main thing is," Dad said, "will he be any good as a football coach? How was his rapport with the boys?"

"Seemed pretty good." Kayla took a spoonful of chili. Apparently, Dad hadn't heard that

Winston Compton, the team's quarterback, had walked out, and Kayla wasn't about to spread gossip by telling him that.

Like most of the town, Dad took the team's losing streak personally. He had been involved in the efforts to hire a new coach. And he was a fixture in the football booster club; in fact, he was hosting a fundraiser for the boosters next week.

Her stomach lurched at the thought of what would happen if he found out the truth about Mike. Dad's rages were notorious. Monumental.

Again, she tried to push the worry out of her mind and focus on the present: the hum of the refrigerator, the steady tick of the wall clock, the sharp, spicy taste of the chili that reminded her of the comfort she'd always gotten from her mother's cooking.

They finished their dinner, chatting about the school, gossip from the diner, and family news. Kayla served store-bought cookies for dessert. It wasn't Dad's favorite, pecan pie, but it would have to do.

Kayla loaded their dishes into the dishwasher and wiped down the table and counters while Dad went out to the living room to catch the news on TV. Dad was great as a childcare provider, but housework was something he had never participated in. Kayla wasn't about to suggest that he help with cleanup, not when he'd done her a big favor in caring for Emma today.

"I'm going to take her upstairs and get her into bed, Dad," Kayla said. "You don't have to stay. Tell Gampy good night, sweetie."

Emma gave her grandfather a sloppy kiss and hug, and the man teared up. He really did love kids, his lively granddaughter in particular.

She took Emma upstairs, gave her a quick bath, and tucked her into bed. Fortunately, Dad had tired her out enough from taking her around town that she fell asleep in the middle of the first picture book Kayla read.

Kayla changed into pajamas and went back downstairs, intending to veg out in front of the TV.

To her surprise, Dad was still in the living room. "You know," he said as Kayla collapsed onto the couch, "Emma was the toast of the diner today. She loves my friends, and they love her."

"Thanks again for watching her, Dad. I'm sure it was the highlight of her day."

"Glad to do it. But the point is, she needs a daddy," Dad said.

"How do you figure that, from her liking the diner?" Kayla ran her fingers through her hair and let her head drop back on the couch. She so did not need this conversation right now.

"She needs men in her life," Dad said stubbornly. "She needs a father. You need to date."

"She has a wonderful grandfather. And I don't want to date." Kayla stared up at the ceiling fan rather than look at her father.

"Well, for her sake, you should."

It had been a long day. Kayla had kept her cool while teaching five classes of tenth graders about comma splices and Shakespeare. Not to mention that slightly awkward training session with Mike and his football team before school. She didn't have much of a filter left.

"Listen, Dad," she said, sitting up straight. "You pushed me into a relationship once before, and look how that turned out."

"It's sad he died," Dad said.

Kayla looked at the TV and watched as a football player ran across the goal line and danced around the end zone joyously. "Yeah," she said, "it's sad. And it was even sadder that the marriage was a sham." She mumbled the last words, too low for her father to hear.

"Don't give up on all men due to the problems between you and Beau," he said.

"Dad, we've had this conversation a million times." He looked ready to continue arguing, so she decided the best defense was a good offense. "Why don't you start dating?"

Dad's bushy white eyebrows shot up to his hairline. "I'll have you know, my social life is just fine. I have plenty of friends, and I'm busy as all get-out working on the Tumbleweed Days celebration. Besides, your mother was the only woman for me."

Of course, Kayla's parents had had a great marriage. Somehow, despite Dad's domineering personality, Mom had held her own. They had loved each other deeply. Kayla wanted a love like that someday. But that would mean dating. Which she didn't want to do right now.

"Tell you what," she said. "I'll stay off your case about dating if you'll stay off my case about it."

Dad grunted and got up to leave.

Kayla hurried to get his coat, helped him into it, and hugged him. "You're the best," she said as she kissed his cheek.

He grunted again, then ruffled her hair. "You're doing a good job, as a mom and a teacher," he said grudgingly.

As he walked out into the damp, chilly night air, climbed into his truck, and drove away, Kayla watched, her mind sorting through all the things she needed to consider as she worked out whether it was right to reveal the truth to Mike.

If she did end up telling him about Emma,

she definitely needed to postpone her father learning about it as long as possible.

On Friday, Mike walked into the cafeteria feeling pretty good. He'd almost made it through his first week.

Winston Compton, the kid who'd walked out of the weight training, had come back the next day. He'd apologized in a cursory way, saying he wanted to play quarterback in the coming season. Mike didn't completely believe in the kid's sincerity, especially since he hadn't come to any more workouts this week, but it was a start.

The clatter of dishes, the sound of students talking and laughing, and the smell of greasy fries and pizza were starting to feel familiar. He had heard that cafeteria duty was one of the less desirable ones, but he didn't really mind it. It was an opportunity to get to know the kids when they were more relaxed than they were in the classroom.

He did mind when students left the tables messy with leftover food, so he stopped and spoke to a couple of kids who were starting to leave without taking their trays and trash away.

Then he saw a table of kids he knew from football practice. Of course, they were eating big plates of the worst the cafeteria had to offer. He stopped by and pointed out the posters about health and healthy eating on the wall. But he wasn't really scolding them, just giving them a hard time, and they laughed back.

"I saw you eating some of this pizza yourself yesterday, Coach," Tyrell Love said.

He held up his hands. "Busted," he said. "A guy's gotta eat."

He kept walking toward the cafeteria's far wall, where his duty partner, a chemistry teacher, stood looking at his phone.

When he passed by the table where Winston Compton sat with several other kids, he saw Winston look at him and say something to the rest of the students. They all laughed.

So he'd been right to question Winston's apology. His change of attitude wasn't sincere. He'd plan on talking to Winston later, but not in front of his friends.

When he reached Dale Barnes, his duty partner, the science teacher fist-bumped him.

"We made it through the week. Some of us are going out after school if you want to join in."

"I'm not that big of a partier," Mike said. "Hang on a minute." He'd noticed Winston getting up and heading for the food line, so he walked over and stepped in front of him.

"We missed you at practice," he said. "I hope to see you next week."

Winston's lip curled. "Workouts are optional, right?"

"Yes, but your participation will be taken into account when we start assigning positions on the team in the fall."

The kid's jaw almost hit the floor. "I play quarterback," he said flatly.

"I know you did," Mike said, emphasizing the past tense. He held the boy's eyes.

Winston grunted and walked away from Mike on the food line. Well, at least Mike had given him something to think about. No matter how talented Winston was, he was going to have to work hard and display a decent attitude, or he wouldn't be playing quarterback.

When he went back to stand with Dale, the guy had a look of surprise on his face.

"I heard what you said. You know who that kid is, right?"

"Yeah. Winston Compton."

"Right, and he's from a family that has a ton of money. I think they made it in oil. I heard it wasn't a good idea to make waves with Winston."

Mike shrugged. He wasn't one to be affected by someone's social status.

"Anyway," Dale said, his tone changing. "Someone's coming our way. Check it out."

Mike immediately saw who Dale was talking about. There was Kayla, making her way across the cafeteria, stopping to talk easily with students.

His heart rate sped up, but he quickly shifted back into professional mode. Would he ever be that relaxed, comfortable, and popular with the kids?

She approached them, smiled briefly at Dale, and addressed Mike. "Just wanted to let you know, I've got a free period this afternoon. Is it okay with you if I observe your class?"

"Of course."

"Great, I'll see you seventh period." She smiled impersonally at both of them, turned, and headed out of the cafeteria.

They both watched her go. Dale's admiration was obvious.

Mike's fists clenched. It took all his self-control not to slug the guy.

"She's pretty. Want to trade mentors?"

Just like he'd felt when other guys had noticed Kayla three years ago, Mike felt uncomfortably possessive. He'd never flown into the same kind of rage his father had always gotten into—the dangerous kind—but he feared he might some day. "Just trying to keep it professional," he said.

"Good for you," Dale said, obviously not noticing Mike's inner turmoil.

Mike was nervous about being observed by Kayla in the classroom, aware that he was green as a teacher. But he was also glad to get to spend a little more time with her before the weekend.

Did her attentiveness mean she kind of liked him? It hadn't seemed that way up until now, but Dale's words made him wonder—made him hope—which was bad, because there was nothing he could do about any mutual interest between them.

No way was he going to risk waking up his bad, dangerous side. The side that was like his dad.

He focused on what he would be teaching this afternoon, hoping he would impress Kayla rather than make her critical of him. Hoping he'd be able to keep his professional side front and center, rather than thinking about how pretty and appealing she was.

Chapter Four

Well, she'd done it. She'd set up the next step in her decision-making on whether Mike was going to be able to be a part of Emma's life.

Observing a teacher in class might not be everyone's idea of finding out what an individual was like, but in Kayla's experience, the way a person taught told you a lot about them. The way a teacher interacted with high school students let you know whether they had good people skills, empathy, and compassion.

All qualities that were incredibly important in a parent. And if Mike didn't have them, well, Kayla had decided that he didn't get to know he was Emma's dad.

Even as she told herself that, an uncomfortable feeling washed over her. Didn't Mike deserve to know, even if he had a few flaws? Didn't she herself have some flaws? Didn't every parent?

She probably should have revealed the truth

to him the very day he showed up at Tumbleweed High.

But she hadn't been able to. She was still hesitant. Still scared, as if a giant predator lay hiding, ready to pounce.

She wanted to be brave, strong, able to stand up to any man, to speak her truth. She knew women like that. Her own mother had been like that.

But Kayla had been devastated by Mike's abandonment, coupled with the fact that she'd discovered she was carrying his child. When she'd come home to Tumbleweed, seeking comfort and safety, her beloved but domineering father had pushed her into marriage with a family friend who had turned out to be anything but a refuge. Her self-esteem, already battered, had been destroyed. She would have fallen into a deep depression, except one very sweet little baby had needed her to function.

So she'd crawled and clawed her way out. She'd been a decent mother to Emma even when her marriage had gone on the rocks just a few months after Emma was born, and she continued to try to get better at parenting. She read books and watched educational videos and talked to all the mothers she knew.

Would Mike work as hard, be as dedicated?

On the other hand, how could Kayla keep her little girl's father away from her? Would Kayla have wanted her own father to remain a stranger to her, because he didn't live up to some impossibly high standard of parenthood?

The bell signifying the end of sixth period buzzed, and she walked out into the hall. Mike was there outside his classroom door, fulfilling the requirement every teacher had of helping to monitor the halls. Since it was her free period, she didn't have to, but if she wanted to gauge how he related to kids, she should watch how he acted before class officially started.

Lockers slammed, and herds of kids passed by, some with their heads down, focused on phones, or just trying to get through. Others moved in groups, laughing and jostling one another.

Kayla heard some sharp adolescent voices from a little way down the hall. Then there were shouts and exclamations.

"Sounds like a fight," she said to Mike. She pulled out her phone and punched in the number for security.

Tall enough to look over most kids' heads and see what was going on, Mike waded right in.

Kayla followed, shooing the other kids away,

ordering them to get to their classrooms. An audience only made a fight worse. This one involved a couple of ninth graders, boys throwing punches at each other and shouting.

Mike walked right in between them, grabbed the shirtfronts of both boys, and held them apart. They struggled like puppets on strings, but couldn't break his hold. A moment later, two security officers arrived, and the kids were taken away.

"You should have waited for security," she said as the bell rang. They walked into the classroom, some kids ahead of them, some following. "Are you okay?"

He laughed. "I'm fine. No worries."

He'd actually handled it okay, she thought. Not only had he held the kids apart, avoiding serious injury to either one, but she could tell the other kids were impressed with what he had done. The students settled right into their seats, talking quietly, some of them analyzing the cause of the fight, others laughing about how easily Mike had separated the boys.

Kayla took a seat at the back of the room and pulled out her tablet to make notes.

At the front, Mike clicked into a PowerPoint presentation and started teaching about the causes and effects of World War I. At first, she worried that it would be dull, but he quickly started calling on kids and quizzing them, the PowerPoint more of a backdrop that helped kids who were visual learners.

The kids seemed a little restless, but that was understandable. It was a warm Friday afternoon. Everyone was eager for the school day to be done.

"Let's talk about men's and women's experiences of World War I," Mike said. "You read about this last night, if you did your homework."

"Women had it easy back then," Hunter Brown said. "No combat. Safe at home."

"They always have it easier," another boy said, agreeing.

"You've got to be kidding me," Lindy Lopez said. She was one of the brighter students, a leader on the school's academic quiz team that travelled to competitions all over the state, and an advocate for the rights of anyone who had been oppressed. "Women's safety is always more at risk than men's. It's at risk from men."

Mike smiled at her. "Excellent point," he said. "Why don't you look into that a little more deeply, and bring us back some examples from this era on Monday."

"Burn!" Hunter laughed.

Lindy raised an eyebrow at him. "You act like it would be a hardship to do a little reading outside of class," she said. She put a finger to her cheek in mock thoughtfulness. "Maybe it would be, for you."

The girl next to Lindy high-fived her.

Kayla watched Mike, wondering how he would deal with the argument.

He took it in stride. "I'm glad to see you engaged with the material," he said, smiling at Lindy. Then he looked at Hunter. "As for you, how about you do a little research on women in combat during World War I. And yes, there were some," he said, raising a hand to quell the murmurs around the classroom. "Bring us enough facts to fill a PowerPoint slide, and we'll discuss it in class on Monday."

Hunter puffed out a breath. "Fine."

"Hey, Coach C, did you grow up around here?" one of the kids from the football team asked.

"Yeah, we heard some stuff about your family," another player chimed in.

Mike's jaw tightened, and a red flush crossed his face. "How about we stick to World War I history," he said.

He went on, using more of a lecture format. That made sense, Kayla knew, because he had to get through a certain amount of material this week.

But his reaction to the comment about his family background made Kayla curious. She'd known almost nothing about his family background when they'd dated before. Was there something to worry about there?

As he taught on, his tension seemed to dissipate. Kayla couldn't help noticing how clearly he explained the difficult material. And how nice of a smile he had. That dimple!

When a photo of a female scientist from the World War I era showed up on the screen, one of Hunter's friends made a derogatory sound. "She may be smart, but she's ugly."

Kayla bit back her own reaction.

"Inappropriate," Mike said. He immediately assigned the student who had made the comment to research the woman he called ugly, telling him to make a slide listing five of her accomplishments.

Kayla approved of that approach.

For the last fifteen minutes of class, Mike broke the students into small groups to discuss the scientific developments of the era and how they'd affected the outcome of the war.

Overall, Kayla was impressed with how Mike handled the class. She was glad he'd put a stop to the sexist remarks, something kids of this age were prone to.

She listened to a couple of girls in a small group talking about how they would rather be pretty than have accomplishments. She couldn't resist joining in there. "It's about so much more than how you look," she said. "Looks don't make for a happy life. You need to focus on what you can accomplish in the world."

"But don't you want to appeal to men?" one of the girls asked Kayla.

"No," she said reflexively. "That's not the most important thing in life."

"Exactly what my mom says," Lindy contributed.

But as the conversation moved on, Kayla realized she may have misspoken. She did want to appeal to Mike on some level. Even though she knew it was foolish to even think about such things.

When the class was over, she lingered by Mike's desk while he walked a couple of students to the door, answering their questions. She'd wait and give him a little feedback. Memories of her first year of teaching came back to her, and she knew she'd always appreciated knowing an observer's initial impressions, rather than waiting for a formal report.

She glanced down idly and noticed a rental application on Mike's desk. Interesting. That first day, he'd mentioned looking for a more permanent place to live.

Scanning further, she saw a section asking about any criminal record.

She gently nudged aside the paper that was half covering the application and looked at the criminal record section. There was nothing listed there.

"What are you doing?"

Kayla jolted. The voice was very close behind her. Mike.

She took a big step and turned to face him. "I...was just being nosy."

"Why?" He didn't sound angry so much as curious.

"There's something I need to talk to you about," she said. "But not here. Would you mind spending half an hour at the bakery with me?"

He studied her for a moment, then frowned and said, "Okay."

There was no going back now. She had to tell him the truth.

"Let's walk over to the bakery," she said after they gathered their things and were heading out the door of the high school. "It's just a couple of blocks away, and it's a nice day."

"Sure," he responded. They made their way through the few remaining students and colleagues and started down the school walkway toward the street.

"So... Did you want to talk to me about my teaching? Was it that bad?"

"What? No!" Kayla looked up at him. "You really did a good job with all of the gender issues that came up. And I liked that you assigned people to do work outside of class. They'll learn something, and those who want to avoid extra work won't make a bunch of silly remarks or ask inane questions to try to get you off track."

"My thought exactly," he said. As they headed down Walnut Street, passing in front of the post office and then the thrift shop, people greeted them. Kayla noticed some interested looks. One student, a football player, raised his eyebrows and gave Mike a thumbs-up. She didn't understand until Mike looked over at her and said, "You know, if we walk around town together, outside of school, people are going to think we're dating."

"Great," Kayla said. "Just what I need." She wanted to explain, fearing he'd be hurt, but then remained silent. They weren't a couple, and they weren't going to be. But they were connected, and the evidence of that connection was at the day care center right now, winding up her day.

They passed the diner and the beauty shop, and at both spots, Kayla wondered if people were looking at them, noting that Kayla Stewart, that offbeat member of the Stewart family who became a high school teacher, was fraternizing with the new head coach. Oh, well, it couldn't be helped.

Finally, they reached the Sweet Dreams Bakery, and Mike held the door for her. Immediately, she was assailed with the enticing aroma of cookies and muffins and sweet, sugary pastries. The place hummed with conversation from locals, several of whom called out greetings to Kayla.

After a short wait in line, they reached the display case filled with rows of cookies, bear claws, and the bakery's famous Texas-size cinnamon rolls. Exercising restraint—and because her stomach was churning with tension—Kayla just ordered coffee. Mike, however, ordered two cinnamon rolls. "One for now and one for tomorrow morning," he explained, grinning. "Living out of a motel room, there's not much chance to cook a healthy breakfast."

"You won't regret it," she said, nodding at the fragrant pastries. "Luna's cinnamon rolls are totally worth it."

They wound their way through the tables, greeting friends and acquaintances.

"Hey, Coach!"

"Hi, Miss Kayla!"

"Miss Stewart, sorry I wasn't in school today. I'll explain it tomorrow."

She glanced up at Mike. "In case you didn't notice, it's a small town, and teachers and coaches are pretty well-known," she said.

Then a familiar deep voice boomed out, "Kayla! Come sit with us!"

Kayla's heart sank. Her father? Really? Just the person she didn't want to see when she was trying to get up her courage to explain an incredibly difficult and complicated situation to Mike.

She couldn't ignore her dad, though, so she headed toward his table. She was surprised to see that he was sitting with Patty Wright, the widowed matriarch of the Big W Ranch.

"Hi, sweetie!" Patty stood and hugged Kayla. "I forgot my wallet, and your dad was kind enough to pay for my muffin and coffee. We've been sitting here catching up."

Kayla introduced Mike to Patty and then hugged her father. When Patty sat down again, Kayla studied her. She was a pretty woman in her mid-sixties, prettier now with her face a little flushed. Why was it flushed?

She hadn't considered Patty when she'd told her father he ought to date, but it wasn't a bad idea. Patty was a kind woman, and a strong one, too. Like Kayla's mom, Patty might be able to hold her own with Dad.

"Sit down," her father repeated. "I want to talk about the fundraiser next week." He looked at Mike. "I'm hoping you'll come meet the boosters."

"I got the invitation," Mike said. "I'll be there."

Kayla groaned inwardly. The last thing she needed was for them to get pulled into a long drawn-out discussion about the football team boosters. "We're actually going to talk school stuff, Dad," she said, "so I'm going to turn down the invite to sit with you."

He frowned, his bushy eyebrows drawing together. "You can sit down with your father for a minute."

Kayla didn't have it in her to get into an argument with her father today. Fortunately, Patty spoke up. "They're not retired like us, Jim," she said. "They don't have all the time in the world. Let them go about their business."

Dad raised a bushy eyebrow. It was rare that someone contradicted him. She was even more impressed with Patty.

Kayla smiled her thanks and checked the time

on her phone. "She's right, Dad. I have to pick up Emma in a little bit, so we'd better get going. Good to see you guys." Before her father could protest, she headed for a table in the corner.

Once they sat down with their coffee and cinnamon rolls, she flashed him an apologetic smile. "Maybe this wasn't such a good idea," she said. "Everyone in town is here today."

"Including your father," he said.

"I know." She let herself be sidetracked, putting off the serious discussion as long as she could. "I've been hoping he would start dating again just to get him off my case. I hadn't thought of Patty Wright. They're old friends, so it's not a bad match."

"Your mom passed away?" There was sympathy in his dark eyes.

"She did. Not long before..." Kayla paused. "Not long before you and I dated."

"I'm sorry." He met her gaze. "There was a lot we didn't know about each other back then."

"There was." She sucked in a breath. "Mike... there's something I want to tell you now."

He lifted an eyebrow. "Does it have to do with the reason you were looking at private papers on my desk?"

She felt her cheeks heating. "Actually," she said, "it does."

"I'm interested to hear." He seemed friendly now, but she knew that after her revelation, nothing would be the same.

She hesitated, biting her lip.

"Kayla." He touched her hand for a split second. The brush of his fingers was so fast, she wasn't sure if it'd really happened or not. "Just spit it out," he said.

"Okay." She took another deep breath and let it out, slowly. "You know when we dated and then broke up?"

He nodded, his eyes intent on her.

"I told you there was a reason I wanted to find you when you blocked me."

"Yeah," he said. "I'm really sorry about that."

Again, she sucked in a breath and let it out. "Mike, the reason I wanted to get in touch with you was… I found out I was pregnant."

He gasped and his eyes went wide. There was a beat of silence. Then, "Did I hear that right? You got pregnant?"

She nodded, and straightened her shoulders. "You heard me right. Emma is your daughter."

Chapter Five

Mike stared at Kayla as her words echoed in his mind.

Emma is your daughter.

Each word sent his thoughts spinning in all directions.

Emma. He liked that name, always had.

Emma is your daughter.

Is. Not "might be" or "could be" or "I think maybe," but *is*. Kayla was certain that he was the father of her child.

Emma is your daughter.

Emma was his. He hadn't had a family member to consider his own since his mother had died when he was ten. Not one he wanted to claim, anyway. His father was dead to him. The idea that there was a child in the world who was his… His throat tightened at the thought.

Emma is your daughter.

He had a daughter. He couldn't quite believe

it was true. "I don't see how that can be," he said. "We were careful."

She tilted her head to one side and met his eyes steadily. "Mostly."

Immediately, memories washed over him. "That's true," he said, his stomach twisting with shame. "Why didn't you tell me?"

"Mike. You ghosted me, and blocked my phone number, remember? I had no way to get in touch with you."

"Of course you could have. I played for the NFL. You could've gotten in touch with me somehow."

She swallowed hard and looked at the table. Slowly, she nodded. "You're right. After the season started, and you were in the news again, I could have. Maybe even before that, if I'd been on top of things. But… I was really struggling for a while."

Struggling too much to make a few phone calls or do an internet search? Angry emotions churned within him. "That's no excuse!"

"Keep it down, okay?" She straightened a coffee cup he'd bumped to the side, not looking in the least intimidated. "We need to decide how to handle this on our own, not with input from half the town."

He took a deep breath and let it out slowly. Then he did it again. His heart rate settled down.

She sat up straight and looked over toward where her father had been sitting. "Good, Dad's gone. But still, let's keep this to ourselves. We need to talk it through."

The adrenaline he'd felt rushing through him was dissipating, leaving him drained. He let his head fall into his hands. "I don't know what to say. I can't believe this."

"I'm happy to do a DNA test," she said quietly. "You don't have to take my word for it that Emma is yours."

He stared at her. It hadn't occurred to him not to believe her. She wasn't the type to take advantage of anyone.

"Were you just never going to let me know?" he asked her.

"Probably not," she said. "I mean, I could've contacted you when you were active in the NFL. But after your injury, you disappeared. I was also busy being a new mom." She looked down at the table again, then met his eyes. "Plus, I... I got married."

This was blowing his mind. "You knew this baby was mine, and yet, you married someone else? And he was fine with it?"

She tilted her head toward where her father

had been sitting. "It was Dad's idea. But you have to understand. I was so traumatized. I was in love with you, and you'd dumped me for no reason I could understand."

Again, a sense of guilt and shame twisted Mike's gut.

"So there I was," she went on, "pregnant by a man who'd let me know he cared nothing for me, all alone in a big city. The only thing I could think of was to come home, where at least I had family who could help me."

He hated the picture her words painted. Hated the story where he was cast as the villain, even though it was accurate. He'd known he'd hurt her when he'd broken it off and blocked her number on his phone, but he hadn't had a clue of the true devastation he'd caused.

"So you came back to Tumbleweed." He hadn't even known she was from here when they'd dated. "Did your family welcome you with open arms?"

"Sort of." She sighed. "I moved right back into my childhood bedroom. But my father is a strong-willed man who doesn't take no for an answer."

"You got married because your father forced you?" He shook his head. "That doesn't sound like the woman I knew back in Austin."

"Right," she said. "I was able to break away from Dad and from Tumbleweed. But when I came home... Well, it's a small town. Faith plays a big role in the community, and being an unwed mother...well..." She pushed back a strand of hair and met his eyes. "It was a mistake, being intimate with you."

"And marrying some random guy made it right?" Mike tried to understand her side of things, but he was having a hard time of it.

"Not some random guy. Beau was a family friend. Who turned out to be a really bad husband."

The bakery was emptying out around them. Chatter had died down, and the bells on the door indicated customers departing. He looked around them. Sure enough, only two other tables were occupied now.

Kayla was studying the tabletop, running her finger over a circular pattern in the wood. Then she spoke again. "I'm sure there are women who are strong enough to go through a pregnancy by themselves. Who can labor for hours—twenty-two hours, to be exact—and then get up out of bed and care for a baby by themselves. But I'm not that woman. I knew I needed help. I knew the baby would be better off if it wasn't just me, and so I came home."

Her words hammered at his heart, opening it just a little. "Twenty-two hours?"

"Yeah. Emma was stubborn from the very beginning." She half smiled.

His child had a personality he knew nothing about. That hurt. But he couldn't just focus on himself, not after what she'd just told him. "I'm sorry you went through all that alone," he said. "I'm sorry I wasn't there for you. But I'm still hurt that you didn't do all that you could to let me know."

"You have a point, and I'm sorry." She sighed. "In my defense, you'd made it crystal clear you didn't want me. You told me in no uncertain terms that it wasn't going to work out between us. And then you left town. So...the truth is, you didn't seem like the kind of man I wanted as Emma's father." She lifted her hands, palms up. "I'm not claiming that I did everything right, Mike. It's just..." She checked the time on her phone, then stood abruptly. "Look, I have to go pick up Emma at day care. Why don't you text me over the weekend about how you want to handle things. Like I said, I'm happy to do a DNA test if that's important to you. And I'm not asking you for child support or anything like that. I just figured you should know. Since... you know, you're living in town now."

"Where does she go to day care?" he asked suddenly.

"Um..." Kayla's shoulders tensed. "Why do you ask?"

"I want to see her." Suddenly, it was all he could think about. He had to see his daughter. He couldn't wait another day to see her, let alone the whole weekend.

"You're not going to try to take her, are you?" Kayla's voice sounded like she was trying to make a joke but failing.

Anger flared up in him. "Of course not! What kind of man do you think I am?"

She crossed her arms in front of her. Suddenly, she looked small and vulnerable. "It happens," she said. "And I know you're not like that, but...when you're a parent, you worry about everything."

He guessed that was probably true. Especially for a single mom. His anger dissipated. "I won't go near her," he promised. "I just want to see her."

"She goes to Tiny Texans." Kayla spoke slowly, hesitantly. "On Stewart Street, about half a mile past the Feed and Supply. You can follow me there, if you want to see her. But stay in your car. I'm not ready for you to meet her yet. She has no idea who you are, and I want to prepare her properly."

"Stay in my car?"

"Yes." She lifted her chin. "You can see her, but I don't want you meeting her until you've cooled down."

Then she walked out of the bakery, her high heels tapping against the tile floor.

Mike stared after her for a moment. Then he stood and followed her as she speed-walked back toward the school.

His head was spinning as he tried to understand this life-changing information.

He had a daughter.

Now what?

Kayla's hands shook as she drove to the day care center.

She'd done it. She'd told Mike that he was Emma's father.

Mike had gotten a little bit angry. She'd expected that. Anyone would be upset to have this kind of news dropped on them.

But he'd also seemed interested in Emma. Rather than pushing Kayla and the whole concept of being a father away, he'd immediately asked to see his daughter. She glanced in the rearview mirror, and there he was, following her in his truck.

Now that she'd told him, what was next?

Would Mike want to be involved in their lives? Or would he ghost her and Emma and leave town?

Suddenly, it occurred to her that he could seek partial, or even full, custody of Emma.

There was no way she'd let that happen. It was bad enough that she was a single mom. That wasn't what Kayla had ever wanted for herself. It was always good to have a partner.

But a good, kind, caring partner, not someone who didn't truly love you, like Beau. Been there, done that. She'd never put herself through that again.

As she pulled up to the day care center, she made a decision: She wasn't going to tell Emma or anyone else about this. She was going to wait to see if Mike suggested any next steps in this whole situation.

If he didn't, that would tell her all she needed to know.

Given the way he'd acted when he broke up with her three years ago, she could imagine him hightailing it out of town. If he'd been unable to handle the idea of a relationship with Kayla, then how would he handle the idea of having a child?

Would he even be at school on Monday, or would he jump ship?

On the other hand, he'd asked questions, and had asked to see Emma. So maybe he actually would be in touch with her over the weekend. If he did, what would he say? What would he do?

She didn't like leaving the ball in his court. She liked making her own decisions. But a baby was the product of two people, and she had to let him think about this situation, then let her know what he wanted to do.

She pulled into the parking lot, climbed out of her car, and walked into the day care center, ready to see her beloved daughter.

She was strong. She could do this.

If she kept telling herself that, maybe she'd start to believe it.

Mike parked at the edge of the day care center's lot, beside some tall green bushes. He was somehow sweating and freezing at the same time.

A bright mural decorated the wall of the center, depicting little kids in cowboy hats and boots. Above the mural was a sign: Tiny Texans Child Center. On one side of the building, a large playground area with swings and slides was surrounded by a safety fence. A mix of minivans, SUVs, and smaller cars filled half the parking spaces.

72   *The Coach's Secret Child*

The sun was sinking lower in the sky, casting a golden light. Parents emerged from the building with their kids, some holding babies, some walking with toddlers or preschoolers. Moms, dads, and a few grandparents, too. When he rolled down the window, he could hear people calling out greetings in English and Spanish.

He could see himself picking his daughter up at day care someday, walking out that door with her little hand in his. He could be one of those dads.

He was a dad.

He still couldn't wrap his mind around it.

His own father wouldn't have done a day care pickup. If he'd ever given a thought to childcare, he would have called it women's work. Times were different now. And Mike would be a different kind of dad.

He couldn't picture his mother here, either, among these working women, some dressed in scrubs, some in business clothes, one in a waitress uniform. Some looked cheerful and happy on this Friday afternoon, while others just looked tired.

His mother had worked sporadically. He remembered that she cleaned office buildings for a time. She'd also worked as a flagger on a road construction crew, a job he had thought was extremely exciting and wonderful when he'd been a little kid and had seen her at work one day when he was riding the bus to school.

There had never been money for childcare. At best, his parents had left him with a neighbor. By the time he was five or six, he'd been a latchkey kid, staying alone after school and watching TV till his parents came home.

The sight of Kayla snapped him out of his memories. She emerged from the building with a little girl holding her hand, and Mike's world seemed to shatter into a thousand fragments, then come back together again.

Emma. His daughter.

She had short, curly brown hair with a big bow on top of her head. She wore a dress—red, with long sleeves—and sneakers on her feet. She toddled along on her short legs, keeping up with Kayla, looking up and talking to her.

This child had existed for more than two years, and he hadn't known about her. Anger started to rise up inside him again, that he was only now learning he had a daughter.

Kayla had explained why she hadn't told him, and it made a certain amount of sense. Besides, there was nothing to do now but go forward.

As he watched them together, his vision blurred a little. They were a family of two, and

Mike wasn't part of it. Was he even capable of being a father? He hadn't exactly had a good role model.

Kayla approached her car and looked across the parking lot directly at him. Their eyes met even though they were half a football field apart.

She stood talking with another mom while Emma and a little boy chased each other around. They were in an empty area of the parking lot, and he could see that both mothers were keeping an eye on the children.

Emma could run, all right. She was keeping up with that little boy just fine. He felt a tiny flame of pride grow in his heart.

Soon Kayla was helping Emma into the car. She leaned into the back seat, probably fastening her into her car seat. Then she pulled out of the parking space and drove out of the parking lot.

Without thinking, he put his vehicle in gear and followed her from a distance. But there wasn't much traffic on the street to hide in. She would notice if he didn't pull off at the motel where he was staying. Following her would definitely be a bad idea.

He turned into the motel parking lot, but he didn't exit his car. Instead, he did a quick search on his phone for Kayla Stewart in Tumbleweed, Texas.

There wasn't much on Kayla, but there was Stewart this and Stewart that. Suddenly, he realized that the motel, like the day care center, was on Stewart Road. Wow. Suddenly he realized that Kayla was from a wealthy family in these parts. Would his daughter even want to know him, given his family history?

Forcing the negative thoughts away, he found an online phone directory with Kayla's address, and headed there.

It was a cute neighborhood. Nothing fancy, which was surprising given how many Stewart-related businesses were in the area. The address that appeared to be Kayla's was a small white cottage, mostly one story, but with an upper set of dormers—probably a couple of attic bedrooms. There were big trees around the house, live oaks, and a grassy lawn.

Houses lined the street, but they weren't close together. Kids would have plenty of space to roam. Maybe Emma would ride a bike here, or play ball. In fact, he saw a colorful red ball in the yard and imagined Kayla and Emma playing catch with it.

He scanned the rest of the street as he drove. Then he spotted something and came to a stop.

Next door to Kayla's place was another small cottage, with a sign that said For Rent in front of it.

An idea sprang into his mind, fully formed.

He didn't know what kind of a father he'd be, but he did know he was going to try his best.

Starting tomorrow, when he moved in next door...

Chapter Six

On Saturday afternoon, Kayla pulled into her gravel driveway with a sigh of relief. Saturdays were busy days for her, like most working parents. She'd cleaned the house this morning while Emma watched TV, then had taken Emma to story time at the library, which they both loved. They had lunch in the park with some friends from the library, and then they'd gone food shopping at the Grocery Spot. Finally, it was time to relax.

"Hey there," came a friendly voice as Kayla freed Emma from her car seat.

It was Shanae, her neighbor from across the street, approaching with her daughter. Shanae was a stay-at-home mom who had saved Kayla's skin a couple of times with parenting advice, and she'd been a doll about helping out with childcare emergencies. Her four-year-old, Maliyah, was a sweet little girl whom Emma adored.

Kayla opened the back hatch of her car. "How's it going?" she asked her neighbor.

"Just getting home from the park," she said. "Gotta sneak our outdoor time in before the rain comes."

Maliyah was already riding a bike with small training wheels. Sometimes, Kayla felt inadequate when she heard about all the enrichment activities Shanae did with her child.

"Maliyah wants to play with bubbles in the yard," Shanae said now. "Want to have Emma join us while you get your groceries in?"

"You are a blessing," Kayla said. "Yes, please."

"Believe me, it's a blessing to me for this one to have a friend close by to play with." For a moment, Shanae looked sad. She had confided to Kayla that she and her husband, Herb, had been trying for a younger sibling for Maliyah for a couple of years.

Emma was hugging her friend. "Maliyah," she said happily, pronouncing it "Mah-yah." She looked up at Kayla. "Want to go."

"Just for a little while, sweetie," Kayla warned her, then watched as Shanae walked the two girls across the street. She picked up two heaviest bags of groceries and carried them inside.

It had been a tough week. Hard to believe

that she'd only just learned that she and Mike would be teaching together on Monday. It had made for an emotional roller coaster. The scariest thing had been finally letting him know he was Emma's father yesterday.

As she unloaded her groceries onto the kitchen counter, she thought about Mike.

When she'd seen him in the day care parking lot, she'd guessed that meant he wanted to be involved in Emma's life. He had been so vehement about wanting to see her.

But he hadn't texted yet, so who knew? He was probably still processing it all. Kayla was also having a hard time processing it, and she wasn't even the one who'd just learned she had a child.

When she went out for the rest of the groceries, a small pickup pulled up into her driveway behind her. They'd run into Ariella Jackson at the Grocery Spot. She'd agreed to bring over an old dresser that she wanted to get rid of. Kayla was going to refinish it when she found the time and use it for a TV stand.

Ariella helped her carry in the rest of the groceries, and then they went back out to the pickup. Ariella climbed into the back while Kayla stood at the end of the tailgate. She looked across the street to make sure that

Emma was fine, and saw she was running happily around the yard with Maliyah.

They shifted the dresser carefully from the truck to the ground.

"So," Ariella said, "I hear from Ginger that you and Mike went to the bakery together after school yesterday."

Kayla sighed. "Of course you did." Ginger, Ariella's younger sister, was known as a gossip. She saw most of what went on in town from the Beauty Lounge, which she owned. What she didn't see with her own eyes, she heard from her clients.

"Was it a date or…" Ariella held up a hand. "I know, I know. Not my business. I'm not a gossip like my sister. But, if you did want to tell me, I promise I'd keep it to myself."

It was a small town, Kayla reminded herself. Everyone would know everything soon, which was a good reason to keep it quiet until she figured out how much Mike wanted to be involved in their lives.

"Not a date," she said. "I'll tell you about it another time."

"Understood," Ariella said.

They were carrying the heavy dresser, putting it down every few yards to rest or shift position, when suddenly it got a lot lighter.

"Look who it is!" Ariella said.

"Why don't you ladies take that end, and I'll take this one."

It was Mike. She shot him a "what are you doing here" look as they moved the dresser inside her house and onto the sunporch where she intended to work on it.

Once they set it down, Ariella smiled at Mike. "Do you always just show up when a woman is struggling, like Superman?" she asked him.

Kayla looked out the window to check on Emma. Sure enough, she was still playing happily in Shanae's yard.

"As it happens," Mike said, "I found a place to rent. So I was in the area."

"Oh yeah," Ariella said. "I heard that you were looking for a place. Over here, though? I just thought you'd live in the fancy part of town, being all NFL and everything."

Kayla turned toward Mike to find him looking at her, then away.

"A house was available right next door," he said. "I'm moving in now."

Kayla's stunned expression would have been funny, Mike thought, if the whole situation hadn't been so serious.

Mike had made the impulsive decision to move in next door, and he still felt that it was the right one. He desperately wanted to be a father to this little girl he'd only just learned was his daughter. And he wanted to be a better father than his own had been.

But he had to proceed carefully. He didn't want to alienate Kayla or distress Emma.

Kayla's friend Ariella had slipped her coat on and beckoned Kayla out to the porch, where they talked, briefly.

Mike would have given anything to hear what that conversation was about. Had Kayla told other people that he was the father of her child? He'd gotten the impression that she kept her private life private. But he wouldn't blame Kayla for confiding in a good friend. And Ariella seemed protective of Kayla.

The sound of a car engine starting up told him that Ariella had decided it was okay to leave Kayla alone with him.

Kayla stalked inside and marched to the front window, where she stood looking out, arms crossed. Her jaw was set in a way he knew meant she was mad.

"What do you think you're doing?" she asked him. "I wondered if you'd even want to be involved," she said. "But for you to move in next door… That's beyond the pale. You should've consulted me first." She was glaring at him now.

"You're right," he said immediately. "I should've consulted you. I'm sorry to surprise you like this."

She frowned at him, but he continued.

"I saw the for-rent sign last night," he said. "I called the owner and talked him into fast-tracking my rental application. We met this morning and I signed the lease."

"So it's a done deal?" She looked away from him and stared out the window again. "How did you even know where we live? Did you follow me here?"

"Not exactly. I looked up your address online." He realized that could make him seem like a stalker, so he tried to explain. "I guess… I'm trying to process this new information the best I can. Part of that, for me, is finding out more about Emma and her life. I wanted to see where she lived."

"Well, now you see it." Her arms were still crossed, blocking him out. "But moving in next door goes way beyond finding out a little bit about Emma."

She was right, but what was done was done. "Is Emma here?"

"She's playing with a friend across the street." She nodded toward the window.

Drawn like a magnet, he stood beside her. He noticed that Kayla took a giant step away from him, but he was too preoccupied with the little girl playing across the street. There she was. The child he'd seen coming out of the day care.

His daughter.

He watched her as she ran around, then knelt beside another little girl and a woman who seemed to be the other girl's mother. "What are they doing?" he asked.

"I think they're playing with Maliyah's new kitten," she said. "Emma wants one, but I don't have the time or energy right now."

I could help. The words echoed in Mike's mind, but he didn't say them out loud. He was sure Kayla wasn't ready to accept anything from him at the moment. Even if she needed help, even if she was stretched thin like so many single parents, he had to be careful not to step on her toes any more than he'd done by moving next door.

He stood there watching the girls play together. Naturally, he wanted to know if his daughter was athletic. She seemed to like to run and jump, although she was more awkward than the other girl, who looked older.

A splash of rain hit the window, then another.

"Oh, I have to go get her inside." Kayla rushed to the door, then looked back at Mike. "You need to go!"

"I want to meet her." He said it without thinking, but immediately realized it was the absolute truth. He couldn't go another hour without seeing his child up close.

The other mom was bringing Emma over, walking quickly with her, holding her hand. Kayla ran out the front door, and the two women spoke briefly on the porch.

Should he leave? Slip out the back?

But he couldn't make himself do it. Couldn't look away from his daughter. So he stood in Kayla's homey living room, its floor littered with a few toys, and waited.

They hurried in the door. Emma was laughing, saying something about the rain, but when she saw Mike, she went still. "Who that, Mommy?"

Mike's heart pounded faster than when he was about to catch a touchdown pass. His hands felt damp, even though the day was cool.

Emma stood there staring up at him.

Oh, how he wanted to scoop her up in his arms. To study her, to talk to her, to know everything about her. Restraining those impulses took everything he had in him.

She was the most beautiful child he'd ever seen—sturdy, with wild curly hair and big brown eyes. Looking at her, he was humbled. This darling girl had come from Kayla...and him? How could that even be, when he was so flawed?

Was Mike good enough for her? Would she ever be able to love him?

"That's our new next-door neighbor," Kayla said, her voice artificially perky. "He helped me move something heavy."

Mike admired Kayla's quick thinking. So she hadn't told Emma who he was, but she also hadn't lied.

"I help Mommy," Emma said to Mike.

"Do you?" He could barely manage to speak, his throat was so tight with emotions.

He loved the way she stood there, looking at him with confidence, even though he was such a big guy that he sometimes scared little children. It meant she'd been raised in a safe environment. She didn't shy away from men, even big men who she didn't know.

"I help clean," she said, only she pronounced it "keen." She made a wiping motion with her hand to illustrate.

"Ah, it's good you help your mom."

"Can you do something to help me now?" Kayla asked her.

"I help," Emma said agreeably.

"Go put your jacket in your room," Kayla said.

"Okay, Mommy." She headed toward the back of the house, walking with a slightly wobbly, wide-legged stance.

As soon as she was out of earshot, Kayla turned to Mike. "Please go," she said. "I get that you want to know her, but please give her and me a little time."

As Mike turned toward the door, Emma returned to the room. Apparently, she was now comfortable enough with Mike to ignore him. "Mommy. I want kitten."

"You can't have one," Kayla said, "but you can play with Maliyah's."

Mike watched the interaction between them, too fascinated to leave. Emma began to pout. "Want now!"

Kayla flipped on the TV and pulled a DVD off the shelf. Wow, Mike hadn't seen an old-fashioned DVD player in a while. Like most of his friends, he used streaming services to watch the shows and movies he wanted.

Kayla opened the plastic case, slid the disc into the machine, and then showed the cover to Emma. "I got you this from the library," she said. "It's about cats."

Kayla was a clever mom.

Emma held out her hand for the DVD cover as a special about animals came on the TV screen. Kayla picked up a grubby-looking blanket and handed it to Emma. The little girl climbed onto the couch, dragging the blanket and DVD cover with her. She settled back, sucking her thumb.

Kayla gave him a get-out-of-here gesture, and slowly he stepped outside. She followed him, and they stood under her porch roof while chilly rain fell.

"I don't appreciate the sneaky way you did all this," she said.

Mike's yearning to be with Emma made him frustrated with Kayla. "Talk about sneaky," he said. "You could've let me know about our daughter a lot sooner. You could've found a way to get in touch with me, but you didn't."

"We discussed this yesterday. I had every reason to think that you didn't want anything to do with me."

"I'm interested in my child," he said.

"We'll talk. Soon. I promise." She turned and went back into the house, shutting the door behind her.

So, he'd now met Emma, he reflected, walking over to his car in the rain. He pulled a couple of boxes out of the trunk and carried them into his new home.

He'd accomplished one goal: He'd met his daughter.

However, Kayla had been abrupt and dismissive with him. Clearly, she was hesitant to let him be involved in their lives. He understood, but he wasn't going to let her keep their daughter away from him.

He'd made a start, but there was still a long way to go.

Kayla leaned back against the front door, her knees so weak that she felt like she was about to collapse. She walked over to the sofa and sat down beside Emma, who was sleepily watching the cat documentary.

What was she going to do now?

It was great that Mike was interested in Emma. Objectively, she knew that. It was good for a child to know both parents. And Mike wasn't a bad guy. He was polite and worked hard at his job.

However, she now faced a problem. Should she try to block Mike from being in Emma's life? That made sense, given his known tendency to bolt from certain situations. But she was sure he wouldn't accept that. If she pushed him away too much, he might even take legal measures against her.

On the other hand, she could embrace his presence in their lives.

But she worried that if Emma grew attached to Mike, he might suddenly decide to leave. That was how he operated.

Also, she still had that foolish, fluttery feeling whenever she saw him. Even today, arguing with him, she'd noticed the chiseled lines of his face, the broad set of his shoulders.

No doubt, he was a very attractive man. She'd fallen prey to him before.

But this time, there was so much more at stake. This time, falling for him would be a complete disaster—not only for Kayla, but for her daughter.

Starting right now, she had to ignore his charm and all-American good looks.

She took some deep, cleansing breaths and let them out. She cuddled Emma close, and stroked her daughter's soft hair.

Emma was the priority.

Kayla finally acknowledged that it might be good for Emma to know her father.

But just because Mike had boldly moved in next door didn't mean that she had to let him be a part of their daily life. She had to set limits.

She was going to figure out what they were, ASAP. And then everything would be fine.

Chapter Seven

As Kayla got ready for church the next day, she tried to get herself into a spiritual mood. It wasn't easy. Emma had balked at the idea of putting on a nice dress. She'd cried and cried, and Kayla had finally given in, letting her wear her favorite everyday overalls, even though she knew some church members would look askance at her daughter's outfit.

Glancing out the window, she tried to focus on the blue sky and sunshine. It was going to be a beautiful day, with the temperature heading into the seventies. She decided she would take Emma to the playground in the afternoon after church.

Just then, a text buzzed on her phone. It was Mike. Do you take Emma to church?

She took a deep breath and let it out. Was that any of his business? She supposed it was. He was Emma's father, so he probably wanted to know if she was going to get a proper grounding in the Christian faith. Yes, she texted back. I take her to Tumbleweed Community Church almost every Sunday. He didn't respond.

As they drove to church, she couldn't get Mike's text out of her mind. Did he think she would raise her child without faith?

The thought annoyed her, but she had to admit, reluctantly, that it was a valid concern. Faith hadn't been a part of their relationship three years ago. To be honest, they hadn't talked about their beliefs at all. Which was part of why everything had gone so wrong. She saw that now.

When she moved back to Tumbleweed, Kayla had gone back to attending the church of her youth. On the one hand, she was giving in to family and community pressure. On the other hand, she wanted her child to have a church home and a religious education.

Kayla was a believer, but the truth was, she was still a little bit mad at God. He had taken her mother too young, at fifty-seven. He hadn't protected Kayla when she'd dated Mike or during her marriage to Beau.

Life had been hard for her—both during her marriage and then as a single mom. Where was the blessing that was supposed to come from faith in Christ?

As Kayla pulled into the parking lot, she waved to her friend Betty Miller, who was walking into the sanctuary slowly. Betty wore a fancy backpack—pretty cool for an eighty-five-year-old, but probably helpful since she used a cane. She watched Betty say hello to everyone she passed with a big smile on her face.

Everybody loved Betty. And Betty loved God. Even though the woman had had a very hard life. Kayla knew she was in constant pain from arthritis. But she still focused on the positive. In her backpack was a collection of musical toothbrushes, which she gave out to children at church. They all loved Miss Betty, who they called "the toothbrush lady."

That was the kind of person Kayla wanted to be. A positive person, a force for good. And here she was, griping about the challenges in her own life. "I'm sorry, God," she said as she got Emma out of her car seat and kissed her. All the difficulties she had faced in her life had led to her being the mother of her wonderful child.

Suddenly, she heard a truck squeal into the lot and come to a stop. Kayla's positive mood dissipated, because the vehicle was familiar to her—it was Mike's truck.

She wanted to limit their involvement with him, but how could she if he followed her around?

* * *

After services, Kayla hurried to the church kitchen. She was trying not to be annoyed that he'd come to her church. He hadn't tried to sit with her, which was good, but his presence had created a stir. Everyone seemed to be enamored with the handsome new coach who'd played in the NFL.

Not her business. It was a luncheon day, and Kayla always liked to be involved. Being a busy, single, working mom, she didn't have time to help out as much as some members of the congregation did. Working the food line at church lunches was a fun, easy way to contribute to church life.

She grabbed an apron, checked in with the other four people in the kitchen, and headed for the giant pot of rice on the stove. She carried it over to the area where the trays were lined up, set it on a cart, and started moving along the line, scooping rice on to each tray.

When she glanced out the pass-through, she saw Mike come in. Tension rose in her, making her want to leave immediately. Except she couldn't go because her father would question it. Plus, she really was needed in the kitchen.

She tried to focus on her work, but her eyes kept being drawn to Mike. She saw him greet

Police Chief Daniel Montgomery, and they stood chatting for a minute.

Chief Montgomery's twin nieces rushed up to him and pulled him toward a table. Suddenly alone, Mike looked around, spotted Kayla, and walked right into the kitchen. With no preamble or greeting, he asked her where Emma was.

She arched an eyebrow. "She's in the church nursery." She looked around quickly to see if anyone was noticing their conversation, but everyone was busy, and people were constantly going in and out of the kitchen.

"Is she safe there?" he asked.

"No, Mike, she's at risk of serious harm, but I take her there every week, anyway." She rolled her eyes at him.

"She just seems young to be left there," he said.

Kayla drew in a breath, trying to summon the spiritual peace she'd felt during the service. "Emma adores Mrs. Garcia, the toys, and the other kids in the nursery. I'll go get her to eat when I'm done helping in here." She looked up at him, lifting her chin. "Not that it's any of your business."

"It kind of is," he said. "I'm her father."

Around them, the clatter of pots and pans, and the sound of voices faded from notice. She met Mike's dark eyes, emotion washing over her in waves. She couldn't believe she was standing here with the man she'd once loved so much, discussing their daughter. It was a situation she wouldn't have expected even a week ago, and she was still amazed that it was happening now.

"I'd like to take both of you to do something fun after church," he said.

She stuck her spoon in the pot and glared at him. "Mike, you cannot take up every second of our day. You can't be involved in every moment of Emma's life."

"I've missed a lot of moments of her life," he argued. "And we're both busy, so this afternoon is the best time, when I don't have any meetings with the players or schoolwork to do. I would really appreciate it if you would do this with me." He looked away, then back at her, his tone suddenly vulnerable. "I want to get to know her."

Kayla went back to scooping rice on to trays. Someone else started adding green beans to the trays. People were lining up outside the pass-through.

She glanced up at Mike again.

He was looking at her with puppy dog eyes. "Please? It would mean a lot to me."

"It has to be somewhere out of town," she

said, keeping her voice low. "I'm not ready for all of Tumbleweed to know what's going on. And I'm not ready for Emma to know your relationship to her yet."

"That's fine," he said. "I understand."

"And could you leave the kitchen now before everybody starts gossiping about us? People will think we're dating each other."

"Is that really going to happen?"

"Hey, rice, hurry up! You're getting behind," someone called out.

"We'll talk after," he said, and walked out of the kitchen.

Kayla continued scooping rice, not watching him go. But she couldn't keep him out of her thoughts.

He really seemed to care about getting to know his daughter more than she would have expected. That was a good thing. Wasn't it?

Except now she was doing what she had promised herself she wouldn't do. Instead of limiting their interactions and keeping her distance, she had promised that she and Emma would spend the afternoon with Mike.

Mike pulled into the parking lot at Lake County Park, about thirty miles outside of Tumbleweed. He felt like he was acting in a play.

After a quick run home to change clothes, they'd moved Emma's car seat to his truck, and his daughter sat chattering and singing in the back seat. He had a beautiful woman beside him. It was like the family he'd always dreamed of having, but never thought would happen.

Family hadn't meant anything good to him during his childhood. His own family had mostly been about anger and fighting and conflict. But later, in his teens and early twenties, he'd seen a few real families that looked like the ones on TV. Husbands and wives who laughed together, who seemed as if they actually liked each other. Kids who were cute and respectful.

The kind of family that did fun activities together, willingly, on a sunny Sunday afternoon.

Above the lake, he parked in a tree-lined lot. They got out, and Kayla showed Mike how to undo the car seat. It was a complicated process because Emma was so wiggly. "Pay gwound, pay gwound," she kept shouting.

Finally freed, she climbed out of the car seat with Kayla's help. The moment her feet hit the asphalt, she started to run.

"Emma! No!" Kayla rushed after Emma, grabbed her shoulders, and turned her around. "Hold my hand in a parking lot," she said sharply.

Emma started to cry. Did Kayla have to yell at the child like that?

But Kayla wasn't done. She knelt down directly in front of Emma. "Cars are dangerous. In a parking lot, you have to hold Mommy's hand." She glanced up at Mike. "Hold a grown-up's hand," she amended.

"I sorry, Mommy," Emma said through tears. Kayla hugged her.

As the two of them headed back toward Mike, a car came screeching into the parking lot, music blaring, the young driver talking and laughing loudly enough that it was heard through the open windows. They were going way too fast.

Mike's heart almost jumped out of his chest. Quickly, he stepped in front of Kayla and Emma.

"Hey, slow it down!" he yelled at the car as it screeched into the parking lot. The kids didn't hear him, but it made him feel better.

The risk to Emma's safety made it hard to breathe. He wouldn't have known to be stern with her. He might have let her run, and who knew what could've happened?

"Our neighbor loud," Emma said.

Kayla laughed and hugged her. "Come on, let's go to the playground."

"Yay!" Emma bounced up and down, but unlike before, she didn't run away from them.

They walked down a dirt road toward a lake that sparkled in the bright sunlight. Off to the right were picnic pavilions and a path. To the left was a large playground with slides, swings, and other structures Mike couldn't even identify. The air was filled with the shouts of kids, the benches mostly full of parents. It was a perfect day.

Emma started to run ahead, then stopped and looked back. "I go?" she asked.

"Go ahead," Kayla said. "Run!"

Emma raced for the slide, her curly hair bouncing in its short ponytail, her little legs pumping. She wore blue shorts and a bright purple T-shirt, and she looked every bit as cute as she'd looked in her church dress.

Mike felt gratitude wash over him. Gratitude that he had a child. Gratitude that Kayla was a smart mom who took good care of Emma. Gratitude that she was letting him spend time with them today.

He didn't even really know what to do. He watched other dads and tried to mimic their behavior, standing at the bottom of the slide.

Kayla helped Emma climb to the top, then guided her gently as she slid down the small, toddler-sized slide. Mike was at the bottom ready to catch her, but the slide was structured so that Emma slowed down naturally. She climbed off.

"Again!" she said.

This time, Kayla let her climb by herself. At the top, she sat, looked over at Kayla, and then slid down, screeching.

Mike hovered at the bottom again, just as a safeguard.

He wasn't quite sure how Kayla had explained his presence to Emma. But Emma seemed to be taking it in stride. Mike knew Kayla hadn't revealed the fact that Mike was Emma's father yet. But Emma seemed fine with having him tag along, as long as Kayla was there.

Emma went down the slide one more time then abruptly rushed toward a group of plastic spring animals, the kind that wobbled when a kid rode them.

"Is that okay?" he asked Kayla.

"It's fine," Kayla said. "Just follow her around and steady her if she needs it." She took a few steps backward and gestured after Emma.

Kayla was going to let him be the parent in charge? Was that wise? Was he up to the task? He hurried after Emma, who ran, awkwardly but speedily, toward the spring animals.

Suddenly, Emma detoured into a structure that looked like a hollowed-out tree. She poked her head out the low window and shouted, "Mommy, look at me!"

Kayla waved back, smiling. She stood there with her dark, chin-length hair blowing in the breeze, one hand in her jeans pocket. Mike remembered the first time he'd seen her. That had been at a park, too, in Austin. He'd caught a glimpse of Kayla reading a book under a tree, and had felt like a bolt of lightning had struck him. He'd changed course on his run so that he could find an excuse to talk to her.

Emma emerged from the tree structure and rushed toward the spring animals. He followed her and watched while she chose one shaped like a duck. Then he helped her climb on. "Hold tight," he said. His heart raced a little. He suddenly understood why some parents were overprotective. His daughter could hurt herself.

But she rocked back and forth, giggling.

Mike was just getting comfortable with her ability to stay aboard the wobbly duck when she grew tired of it and climbed off. As she started to run back toward the slides, she tripped and fell onto the mulch-covered ground.

Mike rushed over to her, his heart pounding.

"Did you hurt yourself? You have to be more careful. Are you okay?"

Emma studied her elbow. "Yeah. I okay."

She pushed herself to her feet and ran toward the slides again. Mike followed close behind her.

Another dad was running after his child nearby. "Hard to keep up with them," the dad joked.

"Sure is." Mike felt overwhelmed. He was part of the club now, the father club.

Emma went down the slide one more time, then zigzagged away from the playground and toward the lake.

From where she'd been standing, watching them, Kayla yelled out, "Come back! Emma, come back!"

"No!" Emma shouted, and kept going.

"Emma," Mike called. "Come back!"

"No!"

Both of them jogged over and caught up with the child easily. Kayla picked her up in her arms. "You get a time-out," she said. She carried Emma back toward the stroller, seemingly oblivious to her screaming.

She set the teary toddler down in front of the stroller. "Get in now."

"No!" Emma wailed.

Kayla didn't seem fazed by Emma's behavior. "I'm going to count to three," Kayla said. "One. Two..."

Crying, Emma climbed into her stroller.

Kayla smiled up at Mike. "Glad that worked," she said. "I just started using the 1-2-3 method. I wasn't sure she was old enough, but she's getting it." She snapped the stroller belt around Emma.

Mike's head was spinning. "Why is she acting that way?" he asked Kayla.

Kayla looked puzzled. "What way?"

"Running away, crying, saying no to everything. Is she upset that I'm here?"

Kayla laughed. "This is perfectly normal, Mike. She's in her terrible twos, and she's tired." She rooted around in the bag that hung on the back of the stroller and produced a sippy cup, which she handed to the still-crying Emma. "Now we're going to take a walk," she said in a perky voice.

Emma drank from the cup, and soon her cries quieted.

Mike followed along as they walked toward a brick path. Then he took over pushing the stroller, and Kayla walked beside him. Trees arched overhead, and the lake shone on their left. The sound of kids' voices from the playground faded away behind them.

So this was what it was like being part of a family. He walked carefully, almost holding his breath. He felt like if he did something wrong, the whole bubble might burst. Maybe this was all just a dream.

But the woman next to him was entirely real. She greeted people they passed, stopped to pat a sweet golden retriever, picked up a colorful rock and looked at it. She was engaged in the moment, full of positive energy and obvious love for her child.

Mike longed to be like that, too. He desperately wanted to be settled, to be a happy family man.

He hadn't known how much he wanted it until this afternoon.

They walked and talked about Emma, her routines, her development. After they'd gotten halfway around the lake, Kayla put a hand on Mike's arm and made a stopping gesture. Then she walked around to the front of the stroller. She smiled, reached down, and took the sippy cup from her, then came back to Mike's side. "She's asleep," she said. "She missed her nap today, but she'll sleep a little now."

They walked on slowly, sometimes quiet, sometimes chatting a little bit more. Mike remembered this from their previous time together: Kayla was easy to be with. She didn't require constant conversation or entertainment, and she wasn't bored with doing something simple. She was comfortable in church clothes or jeans, comfortable in her own skin.

She was the same person she'd been three years ago. And yet, she was also totally different. She'd been through a lot since they'd known each other in Austin. Kayla had become a teacher, a wife, a mother. He found that he wanted to know her better, wanted to understand the woman she'd become.

"Does Emma remember your husband?" he asked her.

"Not really." Kayla slowed and checked on Emma again. "She wasn't even two when he died, and kids tend to live in the moment. She knows she had a daddy, and that he died."

Mike's gut twisted. He was her father. Would Emma understand that, believe it, accept it? "You said the marriage was a mistake?"

She nodded, then glanced over at him. "Beau didn't love me, and wasn't really even attracted to me, beyond the fact that I was younger than him."

Mike blinked. "Then why did he marry you?"

"For my dad's money."

"Wait a minute. Your dad gave him money when he married you?"

"It was more that Dad bought us a house and cars and paid off Beau's debts, not that he handed over a lump sum to him."

Mike couldn't believe what he was hearing. Who paid someone to marry their daughter in this day and age? And who married solely for money?

"That must have been hard to deal with."

"Yeah. If I'd been in my right mind, I'd never have agreed to it. But I was upset and confused, so I listened to my dad. He said a baby needed a father, and that Beau and I would come to love each other." She shrugged. "That didn't happen."

"So...you didn't love him, either?"

She shook her head. "Honestly, I think I could have come to care for him if he'd treated me and Emma well, but he didn't."

"Did he hurt you?" Mike's fists clenched.

"No, not physically. He was hard on my self-esteem. Emma, he mostly ignored."

Mike took deep breaths to calm his anger. "He sounds like a real jerk."

"We both made a mistake, getting married." She walked forward to check on Emma again.

He couldn't stop himself from asking, "How did he die?"

"You're full of questions today." She walked

a little faster, and Mike lengthened his steps to keep up, pushing the stroller in front of him.

A couple of ducks flew overhead, quacking as they skidded into the lake. On the shoreline, a little boy threw breadcrumbs from a bag, laughing and shouting as more ducks rushed to eat the food. Behind him, a father and mother watched, smiling, holding hands.

"He was in a car accident," Kayla said, capturing his attention again. "Ran his car into a tree in the middle of the night. He'd started hanging around with friends who partied too much, and he didn't handle alcohol well. That night, it caught up with him."

"I'm sorry," Mike said automatically.

"Thanks. It was a rough time."

Her quiet words hit home. Mike considered what it must have been like for her. Getting word in the middle of the night that her husband had died. Going through a funeral. Explaining it all to her toddler, who couldn't possibly understand. Even if she hadn't loved the man, even if it had been a bad marriage, it had to have been difficult.

"Anyway," she said, "my dad helped, and my brother and sister came home and spent time with us, and I had friends by my side. We got through it."

They were coming to the end of the path, back to where they'd started. "How is your family going to react to finding out I'm Emma's dad?" he asked her.

She sighed. "It'll be rough at first, with my father especially." She looked up at him. "That's why I'd rather we hold off a little longer on telling people. Emma can't deal with everything at once, and to be honest, neither can I."

"Of course," he said. "I'm just grateful you let me get to know her a little."

She gave him a sideways look. "You wouldn't take no for an answer," she said, a smile in her voice.

"Guilty as charged," he tried to joke. "We didn't know each other very well…before," he said. "I'd do things a lot differently now."

She looked at him quizzically as they walked, inviting him to say more.

"I was so attracted to you physically. I let that guide me when I shouldn't have."

She didn't say anything.

"What's wrong?"

She glared at him. "Think about what you just said. 'I used to be attracted to you, but it was only physical, so we shouldn't have gotten together.'"

"That's not what I meant!"

"It's what you said!"

Another couple passed them and looked back, curiously, and Mike realized they were being too loud. "No, it isn't what I said," he stated more quietly. "Or at least, it's not what I meant. I was attracted to you on a lot of different levels." He debated admitting that he still was attracted to her but decided against it.

"I liked so many things about you, but I realize now that I didn't take the time to really get to know you. Just as an example, I had no idea you came from money. And I didn't tell you that I grew up dirt-poor."

"Does that matter?"

"It shouldn't, but it usually does." Mike had found that out the hard way. Back in college, he'd had women break up with him once they realized he didn't have the money to take them on a fancy date. Later, when he'd started making good money in the NFL, he'd had women chase him exclusively for that reason.

"Yeah, I get it. That's why I try to keep my family's wealth under wraps. People act different when they know about it."

He nodded. "But I want you to know that I'm not saying it was all a mistake." He gestured toward Emma, still sleeping in her stroller. "A child is never a mistake. I'm just sorry you had to suffer through so much of it alone."

"I agree we should have done things differently, but it's all water under the bridge now."

Their steps slowing down, Mike felt like there was a little more understanding between them. "I just... This is all new to me. I really, really want to be a good father, but it'll take a while till I get the hang of it."

Later on, as they loaded a sleepy Emma and her things into the car, Mike realized that was the understatement of the year.

Because being a good father to Emma also meant figuring out how to co-parent with Kayla. That wouldn't be easy when he had so many conflicting feelings about her. Including an attraction he couldn't allow himself to express, let alone act on.

Chapter Eight

Kayla dismissed her last class on Tuesday and heaved a sigh of relief. It had been a long day, and the kids had been extra rowdy for some reason.

She walked around the classroom, straightening the room up. The smell of disinfectant mingled with the air fresheners she'd placed around the room and the food someone had brought in. Out in the hall, she could hear kids chatting happily.

Kayla listened for sounds from Mike's room next door. When she heard his rumbling voice, she scolded herself. She wasn't supposed to be paying that much attention to him.

But it was hard when they had spent that special time together on Sunday afternoon. She hadn't been able to stop thinking about Mike and Emma together. It had really been lovely, and Emma had talked about Mike nonstop ever since. She had even tried to get his attention, knocking on the window to catch his eye when she'd seen him next door.

Kayla was going to have to tell Emma soon.

She was starting to imagine a future where Emma had a father nearby who could help her develop and grow. She could have a daddy like other kids did.

A dad who was the high school football coach and a leader in town.

She smiled, thinking of how Mike had looked picking Emma up when she'd fallen down, how he'd laughed as she climbed the play structures. Such a strong, handsome man.

This is about Emma, not about you. Kayla knew that men weren't reliable. She had plenty of evidence of that in her life. But she was starting to think that Mike might be able to play a real role in Emma's life. And because of that, she wanted Mike to make a success of his teaching and coaching job.

She was beginning to hope he'd stay in Tumbleweed.

Just then, a shout came from the hall outside her classroom.

She rushed out and found Winston Compton looming over the football team's scrawny kicker, who was trying to get things out of his locker. "Nice jeans," Winston was saying in a sarcastic voice. "Real stylin' hair, too." He rubbed a hand over the boy's head, further rumpling the his already unkempt hair.

Other kids stood nearby, watching. Some of the wealthier kids, whom Kayla knew were Winston's friends, were laughing. Others watched, wide-eyed. Kayla noticed a couple of football players standing by, not interfering but not laughing, either.

"Okay, everybody, move along," she said in her sternest teacher voice.

Winston ignored her. Most of the watchers did, too.

The hallway felt hotter than usual, probably because there were too many teens crowded into too small of a space. "Winston Compton," she said. "Move along. This isn't your locker area. You don't need to be here."

Murmurs from one side of the crowd brought her attention to Tyrell Love, who was coming down the hall double-time, looking mad.

This was going to get out of hand fast, and there wasn't time to call security. "Mike," she yelled. "We need you out here."

Mike quickly emerged from his classroom. She pointed toward Tyrell, whose angry expression and clenched fists suggested he was most likely to initiate physical violence. Then she planted herself between the kicker and Winston. "Get your things and go on to the weight room," she said to the kicker, then turned to face Winston head-on. "You heard me before. You don't need to be here."

Behind her, she could hear the kicker talking with a couple of his teammates, which was unfortunate. Winston wasn't going to want to leave if his target was still here. Instead, he glanced around at his audience, puffed up his shoulders, and lifted his chin.

She could see that Mike was talking with Tyrell, and she heard him utter the word *patience*.

"Go on, the rest of you. Get to your activities or your buses, or I'll start passing out detention slips." She glared around the crowd, and several of the other kids who had been watching finally walked away down the hall.

Winston shoved past her, nearly knocking her off her feet, and began to taunt the kicker again.

"Watch out for Ms. Stewart," she heard Tyrell say as she fell against a locker then straightened up.

Suddenly, Mike was next to her, studying her anxiously, a large, strong hand on her shoulder. "You okay?"

"I'm fine." Aside from a likely bruise where her forearm had encountered the lockers.

Mike nodded, then turned to Winston, looming over him. "You're off the team."

Silence fell over the assembled kids, then murmurs and exclamations broke out. Winston wasn't exactly popular, but he was admired for his football talent and feared for his bullying.

Winston's mouth dropped open, and his forehead wrinkled. "You can't do that."

"I just did," Mike said. He stood in a wide-legged stance, arms crossed, jaw tight.

"But I'm the quarterback." Winston's voice squeaked on the last word.

"Not anymore." Mike sounded regretful now. "You were warned about bullying, and you made a choice to continue doing it. Not to mention that you just shoved a teacher. That's unacceptable."

Winston strode off in anger.

Kayla swallowed hard. Winston deserved to be punished. The school had a zero tolerance policy on bullying. But in Tumbleweed, getting kicked off the football team was a big deal.

"You're sure you're okay?" Mike asked.

"I'm fine," she said. "Let's get this group broken up."

As Mike ordered the gathered group of kids to move on to their after-school activities, another teacher pulled Kayla aside. "Mike just made a big mistake," she said. "He should never have kicked the star quarterback off the team."

"Winston Compton is a bully. It's about time he got his comeuppance," she said, defending Mike's decision.

"Of course you'd think so," the other teacher said, raising an eyebrow. "I heard our new coach moved in right next door to you."

Kayla groaned inwardly. As she had feared, gossip was already swirling around them.

This decision could have serious consequences for Mike. Kayla might think he'd done the right thing, but this town was wild about football and desperately wanted their high school to win games. Without Winston Compton, that was now in question.

On Friday night, Mike stopped his truck in front of a huge home and checked the address he'd been given. This was Jim Stewart's place?

He drove up a grand circular driveway lined with live oak trees and followed a uniformed attendant's directions to a parking spot. Then he turned off the truck and sat a moment, surveying the scene.

The sprawling mansion was set on an acre of landscaped grounds, its limestone exterior accented with wrought iron balconies and large arched windows. A stone veranda overlooked the front lawn.

People were parking all around him, their vehicles high-end, their clothes the kind of casual that cost a lot of money.

Mike's own truck was pretty nice, too. He could've lived on this side of town if he wanted; unlike some of his friends, he'd saved a lot of his NFL salary, and he was fine financially. But though you could take the boy out of poverty, you couldn't take the fear of poverty out of the boy. He still preferred to live modestly and work for a living.

He checked his shave in the rearview mirror, put on his game face, then compared his clothes to those of the other guests emerging from their cars. Yes, chinos and a dress shirt would fit in just fine.

This event was billed as a party, but for him it was work. As the new high school coach meeting a bunch of football boosters for the first time, he needed to deliver a stellar performance.

Besides, Kayla would be here. He definitely wanted to look like a winner in front of her.

The thought of seeing Kayla tonight warmed him against the slight February chill as he followed other newly arrived guests to the tent behind the house. It was huge, and there were heaters everywhere. He heard country music playing—he couldn't tell if it was coming from speakers or a band. Up on the patio, chefs in tall white hats worked the grills at a large outdoor kitchen.

The barbecue smelled amazing, and Mike's stomach growled. There was nothing like Texas barbecue.

He greeted his host, and Jim Stewart looked him up and down. "Welcome," he said, shaking Mike's hand. "Glad you could make it." He smiled, then turned to greet another new arrival.

Mike made his way through the crowd, greeting people and introducing himself. Pretty quickly, he realized that everyone knew who he was already.

That was a small town for you. The new football coach at Tumbleweed High was something to talk about, and someone to meet. A couple of women smiled at him, and several men told him of their own successes on the high school football field.

Mike listened with interest. For some people, high school sports were formative, a huge part of their identity. That was one reason he'd wanted to coach. It could make a difference in people's lives, on and off the playing field.

A couple of guys outright boasted about the athletes they'd been back in the day, and the eye rolls of their wives and friends nearby suggested the behavior happened often.

Jim Stewart had played college ball in Division I. But Mike only knew that from the research he'd done prior to his job interview. Jim never seemed to mention his achievements on the field.

When Jim had a free moment, Mike approached him. "Anyone in particular you want me to meet?"

"Before last week, I would've said Winston Compton's family, but they weren't able to attend." He raised an eyebrow. "Withdrew the donation they'd pledged, too."

Mike had expected there to be talk of his controversial decision to kick Compton off the team. He hadn't considered that the Compton family might be important donors. "I'm sorry to hear that," he said, meaning it. "And I'm disappointed to have had to take that drastic of an action with him. From the films I saw, he's talented."

"You'll find you're not the only disappointed one." Jim punched his shoulder gently. "Chin up. That whole family has an attitude. And maybe some other kid needs a chance at being the signal-caller." Jim turned toward someone calling his name, then turned back. "Make sure you try the pecan pie. Best thing on the dessert table."

"Will do." Glad that Jim seemed supportive, Mike made his way around the tent, trying to chat in a friendly way with everyone.

He didn't mind working the room. High school teams, especially, needed extra financial support if they were going to have the equipment they required. Back in the day, Mike had benefited from boosters that had provided uniforms, equipment, and cleats to kids who couldn't afford them. So in a way, he felt like he was just giving back.

The guests were nice people, by and large. Mostly wealthy, judging by their designer clothes and confident attitudes, but there were some more humble-looking people in attendance, too, including one man Mike knew was a custodian at the school and an avid football fan. Mike liked Jim for including a wide range of people, not just the upper crust of the town.

A few folks made comments about the quarterback situation, but most asked him how he was liking Tumbleweed, whether he'd found a place to live, how the team was shaping up. Good talk with good folks. He got a plate full of barbecue that was fall-off-the-bone tender, along with a few sides. He'd have liked to eat three platefuls, but this wasn't the occasion to be a glutton.

In between chatting with guests, his eyes scanned the room. Where was Kayla?

Just then he saw her, talking and laughing with a group of guests.

She wore a bright pink dress, and shoes that made her taller. Her legs were bare. Her hair swung, perfect and shiny, and her smile was even prettier and wider than usual.

How could a woman so beautiful be so down-to-earth and kind and hardworking?

He was falling for her.

Which wasn't good. Don't forget where you came from, he told himself. Don't get attached. Keep your distance.

She spotted him and walked over. Something flowery and sweet floated on the evening breeze, and all his good intentions flew away.

"Are you having fun?" she asked. "Did you have something to eat? Sorry I haven't been out here much. We had a slight disaster in the kitchen, but it's all good now."

It made sense. Jim's wife, Kayla's mother, had passed away. And Kayla was playing hostess for her dad at this event.

He was starting to see that Kayla had a lot of responsibilities.

"I'm doing fine," he told her. "Nice place," he added with a meaningful glance at the mansion.

"Thanks," she said. "It's great for parties."

"Did you grow up here?"

"I did," she said, but she didn't elaborate further.

He studied her. "I'll admit, I'm confused. Your family has all this, and yet you're a teacher with your kid in day care?"

Two spots of red appeared on her cheeks. She squared her shoulders. "Don't you even start with that."

"Sorry, sorry," he said quickly. It sounded like he'd hit a sore spot. "You're great at your jobs, as a teacher and a mom."

She studied him, eyes narrowed, like she was looking for sarcasm that wasn't there. Then her shoulders relaxed. "I know," she said, grinning at him. A dimple that he had rarely seen emerged in her cheek, and her eyes sparkled with laughter.

Then a more serious expression crossed her face. "Dad's always bugging me to come home and let him support us," she explained. "I would rather be on my own."

A whole new set of thoughts flashed through

Mike's mind. Would he want her to stay home with their child? Would she listen to him if he did?

Of course she wouldn't, and that was fine.

Why was he even thinking about that when he wasn't ever, ever going to be in a position to discuss things like that with her?

Although maybe, even though he couldn't be in a relationship with her, he could help. Should help. He'd learned about Emma's existence almost two weeks ago. It was time for him to support his own child. "Earth to Mike," she said.

"Sorry, sorry," he said again. "Didn't mean to space out."

"Can I get you anything?" she asked.

"No, no thanks. I'll grab a Coke later."

Suddenly, Kayla went alert, looking at something across the tent from them.

Mike looked in the same direction but couldn't see anything unusual. "What's the matter?" he asked.

"My dad," she said slowly. "I haven't seen him look that way for…for a long time."

"What way?" He looked over at Jim Stewart, who was smiling broadly.

"Just…happy to see someone." She stood up on her tiptoes. "He lit up. Who is he looking at?"

Because of his height, Mike could see over everyone's heads. "A lady about his age," he said. "Kind of small like you, hair about as long as yours, too," he added, touching his shoulder to indicate length, "but silver. In fact, I think it's that woman he was sitting with at the coffee shop."

"Patty Wright," she said. "Huh. I wonder..." She broke off and shrugged. "He says he doesn't want to date, that it's too soon. But maybe he'll change his mind. It's been more than three years."

"Would that bother you?" Mike knew that a lot of adult kids didn't like the idea of their parents finding a new partner.

"It would be weird, but I do want Dad to be happy." She flashed a grin. "And maybe he'd stop trying to manage my life if he had more of a life of his own."

It was an interesting statement, but Mike didn't have time to question her further. A man was marching toward them, nostrils flaring like a bull. "You're the new coach," he said. "What were you thinking, kicking our quarterback off the team?" His face was red, his arms akimbo, his legs wide. It was a fighting stance.

"Just a coaching decision," Mike said evenly. He kept his own body relaxed. No way was he getting into something physical with this man at this event.

A woman came over, her blond hair done up big, her makeup applied with a heavy hand. "Now, John," she said, putting her hand on the belligerent man's arm. "What are you going on about?"

"Just trying to figure out what our new coach is doing." His voice got louder as he spoke, his face redder. Mike's nonreaction seemed to be bothering him.

"Settle down, John," the woman said quietly, her manicured fingers digging into the man's arm. "This isn't the time or the place."

Heads swiveled in their direction, curiosity obviously warring with manners. Mike needed to end this. "I always welcome feedback from the community," he said, "especially from our boosters. Give me a call next week and we can discuss any concerns you have." He was pretty sure the man wouldn't remember this conversation, and no way was Mike changing his mind about Winston Compton. But right now, he just wanted to tamp down the fire.

The man sputtered to his wife, but she ignored him. Instead, she looked at Kayla, a questioning look on her face. "I heard you've been leaping to the coach's defense," she said, nodding at Mike.

Kayla looked embarrassed, at a loss for words.

Mike didn't like seeing her that vulnerable. He had to do something. As the woman started to say more, he jumped in. "Sorry to interrupt," he said. "But I think your father needs you, Kayla." He gestured toward Jim Stewart.

"Thanks, I'll go see what he wants," Kayla said, meeting his eyes for the briefest moment, flashing a thank-you.

He wanted to walk beside her, put an arm around her, make sure the lady didn't continue bothering her, but he didn't want to feed the gossip. He didn't like the way people were looking from him to Kayla to the still-angry man.

As he extricated himself from the irritated guy and his wife and continued socializing, he wondered if this event had been a success…or a disaster?

One thing was for sure: He didn't like having to pretend in front of all of these people that his connection to Kayla was brand new and just professional. Especially since the truth would come out soon.

No doubt, revealing that he was Emma's father would raise eyebrows, and it might arouse anger among Kayla's family. Even professionally, people might think he'd come here only to be near his child, when in reality, he'd had no idea that he had a child in Tumbleweed, Texas.

There would be fallout, for sure. But the longer they waited, the more consequences there would be.

As soon as he got a moment away from people, he pulled out his phone and texted Kayla. Let's tell Emma and then everyone else the truth soon.

An answer buzzed in a moment later. How soon?

Let's do it tomorrow.

Chapter Nine

The day after the party, Kayla was moving slowly in the kitchen. She'd stayed late at her father's to help the caterers clean up and to discuss the event with her dad. The whole time, Mike's suggestion that they tell Emma the truth today had been humming in the back of her mind. That had continued throughout the night, resulting in very little sleep.

She rinsed her cereal bowl and put it in the dishwasher. Mike's presence at the party had been a good thing. He was personable and had probably gotten some additional support for the football team from the party guests. Her dad had been happy with the event and had thought Mike's presence was an asset. Kayla had to admit to herself that she'd liked having him there.

But his presence had also made things difficult. Several people had asked her how she liked living next door to him. Clearly, the news that they were neighbors was all over town.

She could just imagine what would happen when the truth about Emma came out.

She put another pod into her coffeemaker. There wasn't enough coffee to deal with this.

Emma, please stay asleep, she thought as she waited for the French roast to spit out. Then she felt guilty about it.

She'd been working all week, and then Friday night, she had left Emma with a babysitter. They needed to spend some time together today.

She started straightening the kitchen just to keep her hands busy and her anxiety at bay. She hadn't set up any weekend activities for her and Emma because she had been so busy with the party planning for her father this week.

But she needed to figure something out. Rain beat against the kitchen window, and the thermometer outside read forty-one degrees. It wasn't going to be a play-in-the-backyard kind of day. Emma needed to keep busy, or she'd be a fussy little girl by the afternoon.

Kayla thought of the library and looked at their website. There was a Valentine's event for toddlers. Perfect. She would fit that into their day.

As she looked at her to-do list posted on the refrigerator, one item jumped out at her: Plan Emma's birthday party. She couldn't believe she'd forgotten about it!

She'd been so involved with her dad's event, it has slipped her mind.

Kayla knew she would enjoy planning a small, at-home party for Emma's third birthday. Once she had a little more coffee.

Emma deserved to know her father, too. And Mike was right that it needed to happen now, before people figured it out for themselves.

Her stomach churned at the thought of bringing this information out into the open.

"Mommy!" The cry from upstairs brought her back to the present, and she hurried upstairs. "Good morning, sunshine," she said, hugging her daughter.

But Emma seemed out of sorts today. She didn't want to wear the outfit Kayla suggested. Didn't want to wear anything, in fact. Didn't want a healthy breakfast. Wanted sugary cereal like her friends ate.

Kayla made her an egg, anyway. But when she turned away from her to finish straightening the kitchen, she caught Emma sneaking a cookie from the snack cabinet she wasn't supposed to get into.

She prayed for patience. "That's a time-out," she said.

Emma cried.

A text message from Mike buzzed on Kayla's

phone. Can I bring something over for Emma? And can we decide whether now is the right time to tell her?

Her heart raced. She'd hoped for a little more time, but what good would it do to wait?

Sure, she texted back. How would Emma react?

They'd find out soon enough...

Mike had been out all morning, visiting a new acquaintance from last night's party and then picking up supplies. Now, he gathered everything up and headed through the rain toward Kayla's house next door.

His goal was to start bonding with Emma. He was pretty sure the gift he was bringing would do just that. But would it damage the fragile bond he was building with Kayla, the bond that would let them co-parent well?

And the bond that his heart longed to expand into something else, something romantic and beautiful?

He shifted the large bag and box he carried into one hand and rang the doorbell.

Kayla answered, with Emma at her side. Just the sight of them together weighed his chest down with a bittersweet warmth. He didn't know what their Saturdays were normally like.

Didn't know if the faded jeans and pink T-shirt were Kayla's usual attire, or whether Emma usually spent the morning in pajamas.

"Our neighbor," Emma announced.

"Come on in, Mike," Kayla said. "What do you have there?"

He stepped through the open door. "I have a present for Emma," he said. "Something for all of us to share, actually."

A tiny meow from the box gave his secret away. "A kitten!" Emma cried out as she reached for the box.

"A kitten?" Kayla stared at Mike. "Really?"

He knelt down and opened the box, and the small tabby crouched inside looked around cautiously.

"Aw!" Emma reached for the cat.

Kayla knelt beside her. "Careful, honey. The cat isn't used to you yet." Then she glared at Mike. "You could have run this by me first."

He totally should have, but he'd known she'd have said no.

"I'll keep the cat at my place most of the time," he said. "When you have the space and time for it, we can share. I bought litter boxes and food for both of our places."

Emma knelt beside the cat and laid her cheek against its soft fur. She seemed to be handling it carefully for an almost-three-year-old, but Mike knew he had to keep an eye on them both.

He didn't think he'd ever seen anything as adorable as his daughter's delighted face. He'd done a good thing, in her eyes at least.

"It's a barn cat," he said to Kayla, hoping to convince her that this was a good move. "Six months old, so not a tiny kitten. Litter box trained."

Kayla didn't answer. She was watching Emma. The cat, meanwhile, crept away from them and wandered around the room, pausing to sniff furniture, walls, and corners. Its green eyes were wide, its ears swiveling as it listened to their voices. "It's cute," Kayla admitted finally.

"One of the ladies at the party last night needed to get rid of it," he said, "because someone in their family's allergic. They just found out, but apparently, it's used to kids from playing with them in their barn."

Emma made her way over to the cat on hands and knees. The cat's nose twitched as it examined her hands. She picked it up carefully.

"Hold the kitty in your lap or let it go," Kayla said as the cat started to struggle.

Emma instantly obeyed, and the cat got itself free, then turned around, bumped Emma's hand, and started to purr.

"Look, she likes me!" Emma clapped her hands, startling the little cat. "I love her!"

"Is it female or male?" Kayla asked.

"Female, and I thought you and Emma could name it. Mrs. James said it's one of the nicest cats she's ever known."

"Well, of course she did," Kayla said. "She wanted to get rid of it."

"Touch it, Mommy," Emma said.

Kayla did, scooting over and running a hand over the cat's back. A slight smile crossed her face. "It's soft," she said.

"You too, Mr. Mike. Touch the kitty," Emma ordered.

So he scooted over and held a hand out to the cat. It shrank away for a few seconds, then sniffed and nudged him.

It was soft. But it was nothing compared to his heart, which seemed to have turned into a marshmallow at the sight of his daughter cuddling the kitten.

"Can we keep it, Mommy? Can we? Please?" Emma begged.

Kayla shot Mike one more glare. "Remember, Mr. Mike wants to share it with us," she said. "I guess we could have it here sometimes."

"What are you worried about?" Mike asked her, worried that she really didn't want the cat.

"Keeping her out of things. Cleaning up after her." She raised an eyebrow. "What's fun for you and Emma is work for me, and I already have plenty of that."

He instantly saw the situation from her point of view and winced. He had added to her burden and put her into an impossible situation, where saying no would make her into the bad guy. Not the best way to start co-parenting.

"Thank you, Mr. Mike!" Emma flung herself into his arms. He hugged her, his throat too tight to speak. He didn't even care that tears were welling up in his eyes, because this was the sweetest moment of his life.

After a few seconds, she wiggled away and followed the cat as it started to explore the house.

"I'm sorry," he said quietly to Kayla. "I messed up big-time, didn't I?"

"Yeah, you did," she said. "I mean, I do like cats. I was thinking about getting her one at some point. It's just, I'm so busy and she's so young. I just don't need another being to take care of right now."

"I get that," he said. She cared for Emma, of course, but also for her students and her father. It was a lot to handle. "I meant it about keeping it at my house, too," he said. "Mrs. James was going to take it to the animal shelter this morning. That's why I moved fast, but I realize now that I should have consulted you first."

They watched as Emma petted the cat, then grabbed a bit of yarn from a basket beside the couch and pulled it along, making the cat pounce. Emma squealed with delight.

"She already knows how to play with cats, huh?" Mike said.

"She loves playing with our neighbor's cat," Kayla explained. "I guess it's not so bad."

The bag he brought over had been lying on its side, forgotten, but now the cat nosed its way inside. Emma giggled and watched, then tipped the bag to make the cat emerge. That led to the discovery of all the cat toys he had brought, which elicited another squeal of delight from Emma. She pulled out the toys and started showing them to the kitten all at once.

"I'll help you clean up," he promised Kayla.

"Uh-huh." She sounded skeptical, then she faced him and pinned him with a hard gaze. "Was this supposed to help us tell her the truth?" Kayla asked when Emma was across the room, out of earshot. "So you're the Disneyland dad, full of fun surprises?"

"I guess. Kind of." Suddenly, the truth crashed down on Mike. "I didn't think she'd necessarily be happy to have me be her father.

But I guess I thought…if I came bearing gifts, it would sweeten the deal."

"Oh, Mike." She squeezed his arm for the briefest moment and then blew out a sigh, looking at him. "This is a mess."

"Should we go ahead and tell her now?" he asked.

"Well, I just signed us up for a Valentine's event at the library. It's this afternoon, and if we tell her now, then take her, she'll tell everyone."

"Why don't we tell her later?" he asked.

She nodded. "After the Valentine's event."

Her forehead wrinkled and there were dark circles under her eyes. Mike figured he was a lot of the reason for that worried expression on her face.

Before he'd come to town, she'd been a single working mom. Not an easy gig, but she'd managed it well, as far as he could see.

Now, she was the target of gossip in town. He'd seen that firsthand at the party last night. She had a new pet to take care of. And she was about to upset her daughter and create more gossip about herself by revealing that Mike was Emma's father.

He hadn't intended to shake up Kayla's world when he'd come to Tumbleweed, but he'd done it. Maybe he could help her deal with the consequences. "Can I go with you to the library thing?" he asked.

"I'm counting on it," she said. "I need help with her. This is going to be a day." She glanced over at Emma, who squatted down by the bag of cat toys, sorting through them again, with the kitten alternately watching and leaping at them.

"You work too hard," he said to Kayla, quietly.

She looked down, and a lock of hair fell in front of her eyes. He reached a tentative hand toward her face, and when she looked up and didn't pull away, he brushed it back. "I want to be able to lift some of the burden from your shoulders."

She looked at him, her expression vulnerable. "Really?"

Again, he was aware of how much his presence had disrupted her life. "Really," he said. "I want to help you."

"That...would be good."

He caught the scent of her perfume and it made him want to stay close to her. To provide for her some of the nurturing she was accustomed to providing for others.

How he was going to do that without falling for her even more... That was going to be the challenge.

But Mike was always up for a challenge...

Chapter Ten

As soon as they walked into the library's children's area, Kayla noticed that several moms were looking at Mike with appreciation. She glanced down at her own clothes. There was a ripped spot on her T-shirt sleeve, and she was wearing her rattiest old sneakers. She was pretty sure her hair was a mess, too. And her face was bare of makeup.

Meanwhile, the mom who was now approaching Mike wore stylish boots with expensive jeans and a pretty pink shirt. Her hair was perfect.

That was fine, Kayla told herself. This was not a date. Mike was Emma's father, not Kayla's boyfriend. Other women were welcome to him. Let someone else try to keep him from running away at the first signs of feelings. Maybe they'd be better at it than Kayla had been.

The stylish mom was talking to Mike with animation. Her body angled toward him; she flipped her hair and touched him lightly on the arm. She looked pretty and lively and fun.

Kayla turned away. She didn't want a relationship with Mike. Didn't want any romantic relationship, in fact. She was perfectly fine single. Right?

Ignoring the sick feeling in her stomach, Kayla greeted the librarian and a couple of mothers she knew. She got Emma settled on a carpet square beside some other kids, and the librarian launched into reading a picture book to everyone.

When Kayla looked over at Mike and his new fan again, she saw him backing away, looking embarrassed.

The woman who'd approached him frowned, pouting a little bit.

Once the librarian finished the picture book she'd been reading, she asked, "How's everybody today? Who wants to hear another story?"

Ignoring the question, Emma shouted, "I got a new kitten!"

There were exclamations from the kids and smiles from the parents. "That's exciting!" the librarian said, obviously used to dealing with young children.

"Mr. Mike got it for me," Emma added loudly, pointing at Mike.

As the other kids commented and chimed in with their news, several of the parents looked with interest at Mike, Kayla, and Emma. The flirtatious mom who had approached Mike turned to the woman next to her and whispered, ignoring the fact that her son had lain down on the floor and was kicking his feet.

One of the grandmothers who was there, Mrs. Smith, smiled at Kayla. She'd been at the party last night. "So, it's true!" she said.

Kayla's stomach churned. This was not the time or place to try to explain her relationship with Mike. She forced a smile and shook her head and backed toward the side of the room where parents were able to sit on chairs. Mike stepped next to her. Not the best way to stop gossip in its tracks.

The librarian got the kids started on a simple craft that involved putting stickers on cutout paper hearts. No parental assistance required.

"Hey," Mike said quietly.

"That kitten is the gift that keeps on giving," she said.

"Yeah, I'm sorry about that," Mike said. "And... I see you're right that Emma would tell everyone whatever she knows, right away."

"Yeah." Kayla looked gloomily around the

room. "Now they all think we're in a relationship."

Mike sighed. "I see that. But you know…you could've told me about Emma years ago and avoided all this drama. And after all, we were in a relationship."

"We were. But we're not anymore." Kayla pushed aside the way he looked at her this morning, the sparks between them. She couldn't get pulled into that again when he was likely to abandon her and Emma again. And here she'd be, facing more gossip about herself and her failed relationships.

"We're still in a relationship," Mike argued. "We're co-parenting."

Noticing that several people were looking at them with interest again, Kayla turned slightly away from Mike and focused on watching the kids.

A moment later, Mike spoke again. "I'm sorry to argue with you," he said. "And I'm sorry about the kitten. I'm just nervous about telling her. Nervous she won't be happy. And nervous I won't be any good at this parenting gig."

Against her will, Kayla felt sorry for him. But her main goal was to keep her daughter healthy, happy, and emotionally safe. How was this new revelation going to affect her?

***

After story time, they walked out of the library to a few rays of sunshine breaking up the cloud cover. The air was cool but comfortable, classic sweater weather for late winter in East Texas. Emma sat down on the library steps, studying her stack of picture books. She was particularly interested in the one about cat care, paging through it to study the pictures.

"Would you want to take a walk?" Mike asked Kayla, quietly enough that Emma wouldn't hear.

"I thought we were going to tell her now," Kayla said.

"I'm thinking maybe we should tell her while we're taking a walk. Might be a little less stressful, and the kitten won't be there to distract her."

That made good sense, so Kayla agreed. Library books in hand, they walked through town to the park. Other people were out, shopping or walking dogs, enjoying the break in the weather.

They reached the edge of the park, and the gazebo in the center of it was visible.

"Zibo, zibo, let's go to the zibo," Emma said, looking up at Kayla, jumping up and down.

"See how fast you can run to it," Kayla suggested. Emma handed all her library books to Kayla and took off.

Kayla and Mike followed behind, more slowly.

"Do you think this would be a good place to tell her?" Kayla asked.

"As good a place as any," he said. He blew out a breath and shook his head. "I'll admit I'm nervous. I don't know what to say."

She squeezed his arm briefly. "I don't, either, but we have to do it. Be brave," she added. "You've done scarier things, I'm sure. Like being tackled by a linebacker. A preschooler is a piece of cake after that." She was trying to joke, but she was nervous, too.

"This is way worse." He smiled, but Kayla could tell it was forced.

"I'll start things off, if you don't want to."

Once they got to the gazebo, Kayla and Mike sat on a bench, leaving room for Emma between them. Emma danced around, attempting cartwheels, climbing up on the benches and back down. Clearly, she had a lot of energy today.

"Come over here, honey, and sit between us. We want to talk to you."

"Okay." Emma trotted and hopped her way over and climbed onto the bench.

When Mike didn't start the ball rolling, Kayla jumped in and began to speak.

"Mr. Mike has been very nice to us, hasn't he?" she asked.

"Yeah," Emma said. "He got me a kitten!"

Of course, that would be Emma's focus. "There's something very surprising about Mr. Mike," Kayla said, taking in a deep breath. Her heart was pounding. She put an arm around Emma. Just say it, she told herself. "He's your daddy."

Emma's eyes went round. She looked up at Mike, then back at Kayla. Then she shook her head. "No. I not have daddy."

Mike cleared his throat. "I am your daddy," he said. "I couldn't be here at first, when you were littler, but now I can."

Emma was frowning, shaking her head. "My daddy died," she said. She pointed at the sky. "He's in heaven."

Kayla's stomach tightened. Of course this was hard for Emma to understand. She wasn't even three yet. Keep it simple, she reminded herself. She couldn't use logic, not really. "Yes, baby. Now, Mr. Mike is your daddy."

Emma frowned. Then she said, "Okay." Looking at Mike for less than a minute, she jumped off the bench. She ran to the other side of the gazebo and climbed on the bench there, stood, and jumped off. She landed on her feet, steadied herself, and climbed up again.

Immediately, Mike and Kayla went to her. "No more jumping," Mike said.

Emma looked at him, wide-eyed, then at Kayla.

"That's right," Kayla said. Of course, Emma wasn't going to accept Mike telling her what to do just yet. "No more jumping. It's time to go home."

"Ice cream! Ice cream!"

Mike looked bewildered, but Kayla laughed. That was the mindset of an almost-three-year-old.

"Let's go home and have lunch. If you eat all your lunch, you can have some vanilla ice cream."

Emma climbed onto the gazebo bench again and looked at them speculatively, as if she were planning to jump again.

Mike glanced over at Kayla obviously unsure of what to do next.

Kayla took charge. She didn't want to discipline Emma, or to have this moment be associated with punishment. So she decided on a different strategy. "Let's go home and see how the kitten is doing. We need to name her."

"Kitty!" Emma cried. She climbed off the bench and took Kayla's hand.

Kayla smiled at her daughter, then looked up at Mike, who was definitely out of his element where Emma was concerned.

They went home and ate lunch, then had vanilla ice cream for dessert, as promised. Then they played with the kitten and discussed possible names for her. When nap time came, Emma went willingly. That was a sign to Kayla that the revelation about Mike was having an impact on Emma.

As Kayla tucked her in, she stroked her hair and smiled at her. "Big day today, isn't it?"

"I got a cat and a daddy," Emma said.

Kayla laughed. "That's right. Now, I'm going to put your music on, and you can take a little nap."

"Okay," Emma said, surprisingly cooperative.

When Kayla came downstairs, Mike was still there.

"How do you think it went?" he asked. "She didn't react very much."

"I think that's normal for her age. She's processing it all at her own pace." Kayla paused. "But she will start telling people, so let's make a plan."

"Who needs to know first?" Mike asked.

Kayla sat on the couch and pulled her knees up to her chest. "My father, no question. Then her day care teachers and our friends. I'll tell my dad tomorrow, unless you want to do it together after church."

"I'm sure he'll want to talk to me," Mike said, "so let's do it together. Why don't I go home for a little while, to give you a break? But is it okay if I come back to help tuck her in?"

Kayla's face must have indicated her feelings and exhaustion about the situation, because Mike said, "I'm sorry." He seemed to read her mind. "I know it's a lot. I just... I really want to make up for lost time. I want to know her as much as I can." There was an eagerness in his expression.

She knew that Emma needed to know him, too. It would be good for her to see him participating in her life and her routines.

"Of course," she said. It would be good for Mike, too. For Kayla, not so much.

She realized that they were going to have to set some boundaries around their relationship. Because Kayla's heart couldn't take this much of Mike's company.

Mike returned to Kayla's house five minutes before the time they'd settled on. He couldn't stop himself. He wanted to be there for Emma. They tucked her in together. Kayla kissed her good-night and then stepped away, gesturing for Mike to sit down on the edge of the bed. It seemed like she wanted to give them some time alone.

He looked down at his daughter. Love washed over him in a wave. It was a different kind of love than he'd ever felt before, composed of protectiveness and worry and delight. He suddenly understood how people could dive in front of a speeding car for their child. Which brought to mind all the scary things that could happen to a vulnerable little one. The world was dangerous, could be really tough on a defenseless child. He knew that all too well. No way was his daughter going to experience even one fraction of the pain he'd gone through.

He wouldn't have believed it could happen so fast, this paternal feeling. And that it would be so complex, woven of concern and determination, yes, but also of tender laughter as Emma reached for a stuffed kitten and sleepily explained to it that there was another cat in the house now.

He wanted desperately to be a good father. To help his beautiful daughter grow up strong and healthy and happy. To support Kayla, who'd done an amazing job these past three years alone.

He wanted Emma to feel loved. And who was he kidding—he wanted her to love him, too.

But how likely was that? He'd had no role models. He had no clue how to be a good father.

Suddenly, Emma looked at him with her eyes a little scrunched, as if she was thinking. "My daddy?" she asked in a tentative voice.

"That's right, Emmy Lou," Mike said. "I'm your daddy." His voice tightened on the last word.

"I'm Emma," she said sleepily.

"Okay, Emmy Lou."

She giggled while studying him.

He had never expected to have children, had never allowed himself to long for this. But all of a sudden, it meant more to him than anything in the whole world to be a daddy to this little girl. By hook or by crook, he was going to do better than his own father had done.

Kayla had kissed Emma's forehead, but he didn't feel like Emma was ready for that from him yet. So he held up a hand for a high five.

She grasped his hand, squeezing each of his fingers, regarding him with curiosity. "See you tomorrow?" she asked.

Mike glanced at Kayla, who nodded.

"Yes," he said, "I'll see you tomorrow, Emmy Lou."

She cuddled her stuffed kitten to her chest and yawned. "Night, Daddy," she said, already drifting off.

She'd called him Daddy. He looked at Kayla, whose eyes were shiny.

As full of tears as his own eyes.

This whole day had gutted him. He felt like he'd run for twenty touchdowns, but still feared what the outcome of the game might be.

He was glad Kayla didn't try to chat with him as they left Emma's bedroom. He ducked into the bathroom for a moment, and got himself together.

When he came out, Kayla had sat down on the couch and turned on the TV.

"I don't know about you," she said, "but I'm just about worn out."

"Same." He sat on the edge of the couch. He didn't want to leave the house where his daughter was. Who was he kidding, he didn't want to leave the house where Kayla was, too. But he didn't want to wear out his welcome. "Should I go home, or would you like some company watching TV?"

"It's only going to be Valentine's Day movies," she said.

"That's okay," he said. "I secretly love sappy movies."

"Then by all means, stay." She patted the couch beside her and scrolled through channels. "Hey, look," she said, leaning forward. "Casablanca is on. That's my favorite movie."

"Definitely a classic," he said. "Not sappy, either."

As they watched it, Mike discovered that they loved the same parts of the movie: the humor, the great acting and writing. It made him remember when they'd dated, that they'd found they had so many small things in common. They quoted lines from the film to each other and discussed the ending, which they disagreed about.

"They'll always have Paris." Mike admired the sacrifice that Bogart had made for the sake of a noble cause.

"That's fine for him," Kayla said. "He gets to be a hero. Meanwhile, she has to go off to America with a man she doesn't love."

As the music rose at the end of the movie, they agreed to disagree. Mike turned to her and took her hand.

"This has been fun," he said.

He felt her squeeze his hand a little and he put his other arm around her, tucking her closer to him. He checked to make sure she was okay with it.

When she smiled at him and leaned her head against his shoulder, he felt like the king of the world.

"Thank you for letting me be a part of Emma's life," he said. "I know you didn't have to. And..." He paused for a moment. He didn't want to ruin the mood, but there was something he had to say. "Kayla, I'm sorry I abandoned you in your hour of need."

She lifted her head and looked up at him.

"Yeah, about that," she said. "Why did you leave me so abruptly when we were dating three years ago?"

He hesitated, wondering how much he dared to tell her. He settled for a middle ground. "I grew up pretty rough. I didn't feel like I was good enough for you. I still worry about that. That I'm not enough for Emma, either, as a father."

"Oh, Mike." She touched his face. "You have so much to give."

He didn't tell her the worst of it. But it had been a long day. He wasn't going to ruin this sweet moment by telling her what his father had done.

She was looking at him expectantly. He drew

in a breath for courage. "This seems like the perfect moment for a kiss," he said, half kidding, half serious.

She met his eyes steadily. "It is Valentine's Day."

He smiled at her. "We did just watch the most romantic movie of all time."

"And we have a child together," she said quietly.

Then Mike did what he'd been wanting for a while.

He kissed her.

Chapter Eleven

The moment Mike's lips touched hers, Kayla was happy. She wrapped her arms around him.

He smelled the way she remembered: soap and spice.

This was sweet and wonderful. The kiss seemed to hold the past and the future, memory and promise.

Then he lifted his head. "Kayla. You're so beautiful, inside and out."

The words were like a balm, soothing the ache she hadn't known she was feeling. He pulled her back into his arms, and she felt…safe. Safe and relaxed and supported, like she'd never felt before. They stayed like that for a long time before reluctantly bidding each other good-night.

The next morning, Kayla got ready for the day in a dreamy, romantic haze.

The air was soft, coming in through the open window, smelling of spring. Looking in the mirror, she thought she looked pretty good. She certainly didn't need blush—her cheeks were rosy pink.

It had been so amazing spending time with Mike last night. She had gone breathless when he'd kissed her, had loved the feeling of his strong arms around her. She hadn't realized how alone she felt, how much she was carrying on her shoulders as a single mom.

Having someone hold her, feeling protected and cared for, was the respite she hadn't known she needed.

She heard the front door open downstairs and tilted her head, listening as she finished applying mascara. Emma was downstairs, already dressed for church and playing with the kitten, whom they'd decided to name Mittens. Had Mike come over? She grabbed her shoes and hurried down the stairs.

She slowed down when she saw that it wasn't Mike. It was her father.

He was kneeling on the floor beside Emma, and she was showing him the new kitten.

"She's pretty. I didn't know you were going to get a kitten."

"Yep," Emma said. "I wanted one, and Mr. Mike got me it." She looked up at Kayla's father. "And guess what, Papa. He's my daddy!"

Kayla's heart started racing. Her father's temper was legendary, and she didn't want Emma to experience that. She hurried into the room as her dad swung Emma into the air.

"You're so silly," he said. He blew a raspberry on her stomach.

Emma laughed. "But he *is* my daddy, Papa," she said. "Mommy said so."

Mittens raced across the room and into the kitchen, and Emma raced after him.

Kayla's father looked at her. "Where did she get that idea?"

Kayla knew that she would always remember this moment. The sun streaking in through the window. The sound of birds singing. The sight of her father's confused face.

"Well..." she said.

"It's not true, is it?" He was studying her closely now.

"Well, um...yes, it is true."

The shock on her father's face was both funny and terrifying. It rivaled the moment when she'd come home and had to tell him that she was pregnant.

"But how..." he asked, staring at her.

"When I was in Austin," she said, "I met Mike, and we ended up in a relationship and... well, you know the rest."

Her father's eyebrows drew together, his expression thunderous. "Did he abandon you?"

How should she answer that? "In a way, he did. But—"

He suddenly headed to the front door, glaring in the direction of Mike's house next door.

"No, Dad, don't. He didn't know I was pregnant."

Her father's eyes narrowed. "You need to tell me the whole story. Right now."

Emma had run back into the room. Tugging at Kayla's hand, she asked, "Why is Papa mad?"

She picked up her daughter, and the heavy feeling of Emma in her arms grounded her. "Sometimes grown-ups get upset," she said. "But you're safe. Papa loves you, and I love you." *And Papa and I love each other, but this is hard.* "Relax, Dad. I have it all under control."

He blew out a disgusted breath. "It doesn't look that way! How much of his coming to town was part of a plan?"

"None of it," she said. "Let it go, Dad. We can talk later when you're not so upset. For now, it's time to go to church."

"I want to know. Now." He took a step toward her.

Her father had never raised a hand to her, but

he was a strong-minded man, and she'd been accustomed to doing what he said.

Except she'd vowed not to do that anymore, not since her father had insisted she marry a man who she didn't love, for propriety's sake. She turned, blocking Emma from him. "You're upsetting your granddaughter," she said.

"You tell me what happened."

She straightened her spine and faced him head-on.

"We're leaving for church, Emma and I," she said. "You can come along with us or stay here. Don't let the kitten out when you leave."

Grabbing her purse, she marched out the door with Emma perched on her hip asking a million questions.

Only when Kayla was halfway to church did she realize she was shaking, hard.

That hadn't gone the way she had hoped. Her father was outraged.

But she knew that he would've been upset no matter how he had found out. He would get over it eventually. Together, she and Mike could handle it.

Mike drove to church in a happy daze. He couldn't stop thinking about the kiss. It had been so sweet to hold Kayla in his arms. He'd wanted to stay like that forever.

Being with Kayla felt like being home.

It did raise some concerns, though. He knew he wasn't good in relationships—not with his family history—and he had vowed never to let himself get close enough to a woman that he might hurt her.

But he felt so much for Kayla. And they had a child together. Could it work between them?

Intending to pray about it, he walked through the church parking lot. Halfway to the building, though, he glimpsed someone walking toward him from the side. Seconds later, something bumped him in the chest.

A shotgun.

Adrenaline surging, Mike looked up from the gun's barrel at a furious Jim Stewart.

"Get in my truck," Jim said, nodding to the side. "We're going for a ride."

It was like something out of an old Western, but Jim was dead serious. Had he found out that Mike had kissed Kayla?

Then he realized: No, he'd found out that Mike was Emma's dad.

Was it smart to get in a truck with a furious—and armed—Texas dad?

He looked around the parking lot. They were running a little late, and most people seemed to have already gone inside the church. But there were a few folks talking in the parking lot, and a car pulled into one of the last available parking spaces.

One thing Mike's childhood had taught him was how to deal with high levels of danger and violence while appearing calm. It did no good to spiral out of control. The panic and fear you felt had to be shelved for later.

"I'm not riding anywhere with you when you're in that state," he said, ignoring the gun in Jim's hands. "I'm happy to drive you somewhere or to talk right here, but you need to put your weapon away."

Jim glared at him. "You talk like you own this town, but you don't. I do."

Mike met his eyes with a level gaze. Inside, he was planning how to punt. His priority had to be Emma, and his relationship with her. He couldn't let Jim try to prevent him from being in Emma's life.

He suspected that the gun was more of a prop than a real threat. Jim was tough and hard-nosed, but he wouldn't really shoot someone, no matter how angry he got. "Put the gun away, then we'll talk," he said.

Jim marched over to his truck, shoved the gun into the rack behind the seat, and slammed the door. Then he faced Mike.

"Little Emma just spilled the beans about who her daddy is," he said. "I want to know what's going on."

Mike lifted his face to the cool breeze and glanced around to see who might be eavesdropping on their conversation. No one was close enough to hear, so he decided to give Jim the basics.

"I was pretty surprised to find out myself," he said. "In fact, I just learned about Emma a couple of days after I arrived in town, from Kayla."

"I find that hard to believe." Jim shook his head, a disgusted look on his face.

"You helped recruit me," Mike said. "You know I didn't apply for the head coach job. I didn't plan on any of this."

"Did you plan to abandon my daughter? Leave her alone to raise your child with no help and no support? Not even a father's name on the birth certificate?" Jim's voice got louder with each word.

A couple of folks from the chatty cluster near the church looked over in their direction.

Mike gestured toward the park beside the church. "Come on, let's walk where no one's going to start gossip. You don't want people talking about your family."

Jim glanced around and seemed to realize the truth of Mike's warning. He started walking rapidly toward the park, and Mike took long steps to catch up.

"Gossip didn't seem to worry you when you got her pregnant," Jim said.

Mike was relieved that the park was mostly empty. They turned on to the walking path that circled around it.

He glanced over at the gazebo where they had told Emma the truth, and his heart seemed to swell with the memory. Wow, did he love that little girl. He wouldn't let anything hurt her. "How much did Kayla tell you?" he asked.

"Nothing," Jim said, sounding disgusted. "But believe me, I'll get the whole story out of her."

"You have a right to know," Mike said, and was relieved to see Jim's expression relax a little. He explained how they had gotten into a relationship too quickly, without knowing each other well.

"I'm truly sorry about that," he said, "and I take full responsibility. I shouldn't have let it happen."

"That's exactly right," Jim snapped.

"I realized we were getting too close too fast, and I have my reasons for not thinking that's a good idea. So I left."

"You left her," Jim said, "when she was carrying your child. How do you justify that?"

"I didn't know she was expecting," Mike said. "Believe me, things would have played out differently if I'd known about Emma."

"It makes no sense that Kayla didn't tell you. Was she afraid of you? Did you hurt her?" Jim's fists clenched and his face reddened.

"I would never hurt her. I know she tried to contact me when she first found out." Shame swirled around his mind. "I'm not proud of this, but I blocked her number and left town right after telling her it wasn't going to work."

Jim looked over at him, his bushy eyebrows drawing together. He shook his head, and they walked on, not speaking, past the playground where a few kids were playing while their parents and caregivers stood talking or sat on the benches. When they were again out of earshot of anyone and walking through a tree-lined section, Jim spoke again.

"She could've found you," he said. "And you should've checked on her."

Mike ignored the reality that Kayla had been pushed into marriage, had been busy with that during the period when she might have tried to contact Mike. "You're right, I should have checked on her," Mike agreed. "I'm truly sorry that I didn't."

"Huh." Jim sounded disgusted, but at least he didn't seem as angry. "What's your plan now?"

"To be the best father to Emma that I can." His reply came instantly, without thought. That was his clear and absolute priority.

Jim was shaking his head, obviously thinking through the ramifications. "People are going to find out."

"I'm sure they will." Mike brushed aside a branch that was growing out over the path, then held it so it wouldn't hit the older man. "It's a small town."

"Everyone thinks her father was Kayla's husband, Beau."

"I understand that you engineered that relationship." Mike failed to keep the condemnation he felt out of his voice.

Jim's face reddened. "Didn't know the man as well as I thought I did, and I made mistakes, but I had to do something."

"Did you?" He couldn't believe that a loving father had set his own daughter up with a loser.

"Yes, I had to," Jim said. "Here in Tumbleweed, we take care of our families."

Despite knowing that Jim's methods had been misguided, the words stung. Where Mike came from, men didn't take care of their families. They neglected them, and in the worst case…

"I have to think this through," Jim said, staring out at the horizon. "Figure out what to do."

Anger flared in Mike. "No," he corrected. "Kayla and I need to think it through." No way was Mike letting Jim take charge of the situation. It was his and Kayla's problem, and it was theirs to solve.

They turned at the end of the path and headed back toward the church building. After a few minutes of silence, Jim spoke again. "There's one thing you need to know."

"I'm listening," Mike said.

Jim stopped and faced him. "If you do one thing to hurt that child or her mama, I'll get you fired and run out of town so fast you won't know what hit you."

Mike knew it wasn't an idle threat. Jim had power in this town. He could do it.

"You understand? Fired. And I have contacts all over the state. All over the country! I can guarantee you'll never coach football again."

That might be an exaggeration, but it might not.

In any case, getting fired and having his reputation ruined would be a disaster. It would hurt Emma, and it would hurt Kayla. Moreover, his football players, who he'd been building a good relationship with, would be abandoned by another father figure who had promised to stay.

His mind raced as he thought about what to do.

"I hear what you're saying. I get it. But you need to know this—I will be involved in my daughter's life. I insist on that."

"As long as you toe the line." Jim was glaring at him.

The words rankled, but Mike bottled his anger. Let the man have a win. "I promise you, I won't do anything to hurt my daughter."

"Or mine," Jim said.

"I'll do my best not to hurt Kayla."

Jim gave a brief nod, seeming to realize that there were emotional waters to be navigated between Mike and Kayla.

They'd arrived back in the church parking lot, where organ music was clearly audible. But Mike wasn't going inside. He couldn't face Kayla, not yet.

Because to be a good father to Emma, and do his best to avoid hurting Kayla, he was going to have to back off from any kind of romantic relationship with Kayla.

There was too much of a chance that he'd follow in his father's footsteps and hurt her.

He couldn't let that happen.

Chapter Twelve

Monday was Presidents' Day, and Kayla was happy for the day off from school. She could sleep a little later, do something fun with Emma…and hopefully spend some time with Mike as well.

She fixed eggs and toast, and then took Emma outside. The cool, sunny weather was perfect for starting a garden.

She tossed a big rubber ball with Emma to get her energy out, thinking the whole time about how to handle this crisis with her father. Since Emma now knew the truth about her heritage, and Kayla's father did, too, she had no doubt that the whole town would soon follow.

She wanted Mike to be involved in how to handle the fallout, but she was unsure of their relationship. She couldn't stop thinking about their kiss, and the promise of it all, but everything was new.

She didn't want to text him first. Then realized that was silly and pulled out her phone.

Just as she did, a text came in: We need to talk.

A slight chill came over her. Yes, they did need to talk, but his cool, matter-of-fact tone wasn't in line with how she was feeling.

She knew it was silly to base her response on one text from Mike. She had read articles about it. Not everyone was keen to use emojis or add sweet words.

All the same, her caution kicked in automatically. She shouldn't give her heart to him.

Too late.

"I gonna dig," Emma said. She had located her little spade and was poking it randomly into the grass.

"No, honey, over here." Kayla led the way to a sunny section of dirt beside the house. "This is where your special garden will be."

She showed Emma how to stake out a section—just four feet by four feet for this first time. They dug a little, and when Emma got tired, they sat down beside the garden. Kayla pulled seeds out of her pocket and showed Emma the pictures of the veggies: radishes, carrots, and lettuce.

Emma made faces when she saw the carrots

and lettuce, but she smiled about the radishes. She liked the bright red color of them.

"We'll cut up some potatoes, too, because potato plants can grow from those," Kayla explained.

"Taters," Emma said rapturously. "I love taters."

Kayla hugged her. "Taters, it is," she said.

They went inside to find the potatoes, and Kayla cut them into chunks, making sure that each chunk had an eye; most of them already had a little sprout. As she was doing that, she realized she hadn't texted Mike back.

But when they went back outside to the garden, he was walking toward them, carrying a suitcase-like package.

Emma hid her face against Kayla's leg in an uncharacteristic show of shyness. Then she turned her face to look at him. "Hi, Mr. Mike," she said.

"Do you want to call him Daddy?" Kayla asked her quietly.

"Daddy!" Emma ran to him, hugged his leg, then ran away.

Kayla had to laugh at Emma's display of confusion. This was all so new to her. To all of them, really, but kids' emotions were right there on the surface.

Mike smiled at Emma, but to Kayla's hypervigilant eyes, he looked uneasy.

He knelt down and asked Emma what they were doing.

"We're making a garden," Emma explained. "We're growing taters."

"Good idea, Emmy Lou," Mike said.

"I'm Emma!" She giggled.

"Of course you are." He picked her up and swung her high, making Kayla gasp. Before she could protest, he deposited her safely back on the ground.

Emma laughed. "Again, again!" she cried, and Mike obliged, making her laugh more.

Kayla was torn between nervousness and delight. She'd heard other mothers complain how roughly their husbands played with their children, swinging them around, even throwing them into the air and catching them. Supposedly, that active style of play was great for kids' spatial awareness.

It was hard on a mother's nerves, though.

After setting an elated Emma down again, he pointed to the package he'd been carrying. Kayla saw now that it looked like a folding tent. "I bought something for the kitten," he said. He unfolded a round structure with canvas walls, about the size of a six-by-six-foot room. "It's a cat pen," he explained, "so Mittens can be outside with us and not run away. It'll work while she's little and can't jump high."

"Yay!" Of course, Emma had to get inside the pen. Then they located Mittens and brought her outside.

It was a great gift, the perfect size for Emma to play in, and she got inside and rolled around with the cat. For someone new to fatherhood, Mike was proving to be a natural at selecting gifts Emma would love.

She started to tell him that, but stopped herself, feeling shy. They stood side by side, watching their daughter, not speaking or touching.

"Sorry I distracted her from the gardening project," Mike said finally.

"That's okay," Kayla said. "I need to till the soil, and that's not too much fun for a child. She'll enjoy the actual planting."

Kayla pulled out her tools and started turning over the soil in the little plot she'd marked off. Mike grabbed a shovel and started helping.

"We need to..." they both said at the same time.

"You first," Mike said.

The sun felt warm on her back. The breeze brought the fragrance of warm earth and wild daffodils.

Her heart raced. Why was she so nervous? She hadn't felt that way before they'd kissed.

Stop being a wimp. "We need to talk," she said. "My dad was pretty upset when Emma spilled the beans about you being her father yesterday." She had sent Mike a quick text about it, figuring he should know.

"I know he was," Mike said. "I spoke with him."

"I was afraid of that. Was he awful?" she asked.

"Understandably angry and protective," Mike said.

"Wanting to take charge, I assume?" Kayla asked.

Mike nodded. "Which I wouldn't allow, but... he did give me some things to think about."

Uh-oh. Her heart chilled despite the warmth of the day. "Yeah?"

"Yeah. Kayla, I don't think it's going to work for us to have a relationship."

The coldness that had formed in Kayla's chest spread throughout her whole body.

"It's too risky," he said. "If it doesn't work out between us, your dad will get me fired. I'm committed to living here in Tumbleweed now, to being a coach at the school and a teacher, and most of all, I'm committed to Emma. That has to take priority."

Kayla nodded. But all she heard was it wasn't worth it to him to be in a relationship with her, to figure out how to make it work.

She turned over the soil more quickly, thrusting the shovel hard into the dirt.

She had been here before with Mike. Had heard him explain why a relationship with her wasn't the right thing. How had she let down her guard after only one kiss?

"Are you sure you'll be sticking around?" she asked, trying to sound casual. Like it didn't matter.

"Of course I'm sure." He looked confused. "I just said I'm committed to being here. I want to build a life here, as a dad to Emma."

She shrugged. "You left before." Her heart was pounding and aching all at the same time.

Emma rushed in and out of the pen, tossing a stick for the cat, who surprisingly seemed to be chasing it.

Men weren't reliable, Kayla knew that. Especially Mike. Why, oh why had she let herself open up to him again?

Because it was wonderful, her sad and longing heart said.

"I'm committed to Emma," he repeated. "I

want to be a good father to her. I want to co-parent with you, just not..."

"Not in a relationship. Right. That's fine." She was proud of how steady her voice sounded.

"Really?" Mike looked doubtful.

"Of course. It's probably for the best. I want to raise Emma to be a strong, independent woman. She needs to see me that way, too."

He tilted his head and studied her. "I care for you, Kayla. If things were different, I'd...well... No point going there, but for what it's worth, you're a wonderful woman any man would be lucky to be involved with."

It sounded like bad dialogue in a bad movie. "Don't patronize me, Mike. We'll figure out how to co-parent and what to tell people. It's fine."

"Watch, Mommy!" Emma stood a few feet away from them. She hesitated, then added, "Watch, Daddy." She proceeded to do a three-year-old version of a cartwheel.

"Good job, Emmy Lou," Mike said.

Kayla's tight throat made it hard to speak, so she pasted a smile on her face and clapped her hands.

Even the cat was watching, peeking out from the enclosure.

The breeze was still cool, and the birds still sang. The sun shone brightly.

But to Kayla, the world had suddenly turned a dull shade of gray.

Mike studied her, then said, "Your dad pointed out that people think your late husband was her father. How do you want to handle that?"

How could he just move on so quickly? Apparently, his heart hadn't been touched the way Kayla's had. She swallowed hard and forced a shrug. "People knew it was a quick marriage and a quick baby. They thought he was the father, though I never explicitly said so. We'll just say it was you, and we won't invite questions."

"Are you worried what people will think about you?"

She squinted up at him, trying to figure out what he meant, and then she got it. "Nice of you to be concerned for my reputation. But there's nothing to be done about it."

Mike stood there uncomfortably, shifting from foot to foot. "I just don't want to make things worse. I'm not sure what to say if people start asking questions."

"How about if you say, 'I'm Emma's birth father, and I'm glad to be back in her life.' I'll say the same. If people ask questions, we just tell them it's personal."

His mouth quirked to one side in a doubtful expression. "Will that work?"

"Do you have a better idea?" Why was it up to her to figure all this out?

Which wasn't fair. She was the one who knew the town, knew how people would react here. Knew the gossip. In fact, despite acting nonchalant, she was pretty worried about how this was all going to go down. Her thoughts were a tangle of worry, but the priority here was Emma.

Not town gossip. Not her hurting heart.

Mike shoved his hands into his pockets, watching Emma, his expression troubled.

"Well," she said, "I'm going to get back to working on this garden."

"Want me to take Emma to the bakery for lunch?" he asked.

"Sure, if she likes the idea."

She watched as Mike went over, squatted down beside the cat enclosure, and spoke to Emma. She jumped out of the pen immediately. "I go lunch with Daddy," she said importantly.

Ten minutes later, Kayla watched them walk away together, hand in hand. Her throat was tight, her eyes wet.

Emma would now be less of her child, and more of his. Kayla would be alone more often.

She definitely wouldn't have a wonderful man at her side.

She finished turning over the garden soil and broke up clods of dirt, then dug trenches for planting later on.

Her thoughts settled into a gloom, punctuated by shovelfuls of dirt. *You can do this. You were on your own before and you're on your own now.*

On Wednesday afternoon, Mike ran around the school track, his muscles working hard. Beside him, Tyrell Love ran more easily.

It was a cool day, and Mike was here to make sure that Tyrell did his punishment laps for an outburst he'd had in the weight room this morning.

Truth be told, he was also trying to outrun his thoughts about Kayla. The way she reacted to him telling her they couldn't have a relationship on Monday morning didn't strike him quite right. She'd acted nonchalant, but she'd also asked him if he was moving away. As if she expected him to just pick up and go.

Of course, she had reason to think he would run away, since he'd done it to her before, but he'd thought he had shown her that he was different.

180   *The Coach's Secret Child*

Mike needed to think the whole thing through. He needed to settle in himself what it meant to be a good dad in the presence of Kayla.

He knew he'd done the right thing by pulling away.

Sometimes, doing the right thing was really painful.

"Come on, Coach!" Tyrell picked up the pace, and they raced their last lap with Tyrell narrowly beating him.

On the field beside them, the baseball team was practicing. The sun was low in the sky.

"Good work today," Mike said, deliberately focusing on the present moment as they jogged a cooldown lap. "Man, I'm starving."

"Same," Tyrell said.

"Is your mom fixing dinner for you?" He knew Tyrell was an only child and lived with his mother.

"Nah. She's working extra hours this week."

Mike looked over at the boy. He was thin, even though Mike had seen him eat like a horse at lunch. "You have food at home?"

Tyrell didn't look at him. "I'll find something."

They slowed and finished their lap. Mike grabbed a towel for himself and tossed one to the teenager, then they sat down on a bench.

"Is there a food pantry in Tumbleweed?" Mike asked quietly.

Tyrell gave him a quick glance, then looked at the ground and shook his head. "There's one in Beaumont, but we didn't make it this month. Car broke down."

That was something Tumbleweed needed. Mike wondered if the church was aware.

"How do you know about food pantries?" Tyrell asked.

"Grew up poor." Mike tossed his towel on top of his gym bag.

"You help your folks out now?" the boy asked. "That's what I want to do. I want to go far in football and help out my mom."

"Keep working and keep control of your temper and you have a good chance. Football can help you get to college, at least."

"Bet you bought your folks a mansion, getting all the way to the NFL." There was admiration in Tyrell's voice.

Mike was tempted to let that impression stand, but he wanted to be real with this kid. He liked Tyrell, and identified with his struggles. "Didn't have the opportunity to buy them anything," he said. "My mom passed away, and my dad's in prison."

Tyrell's eyebrows shot up. "Same," he said. "Ever since I was ten. It stinks."

"The other kids tease you?"

"Some. That's why I was mad this morning. You?"

"Yeah. I tried to keep it a secret, but it always seemed to get out."

They sat quietly for a few minutes. Mike had never thought anything good could come out of his family situation, but maybe he was wrong.

"Everybody thinks I'm gonna follow in his footsteps," Tyrell said.

Mike nodded. "I know how it is. The way people react always made me mad, too, but I learned how to breathe. And I did some praying, too, but that came later."

"You learned how to breathe?" Tyrell frowned at him like he'd said something foolish.

"Yep." He demonstrated the breathing technique he'd learned from his final, best foster family. "Breathe in on a count of three. Hold it. Breathe out on a count of four. Hold it. Do that three or four times. When I get mad, that's what I do."

"I've seen you do it," Tyrell said.

Mike nodded. "On a daily basis."

"You get mad every day?"

Mike smiled. "Pretty much."

Tyrell propped his elbows on his knees and clasped his hands. "Man, I thought I was the only one."

"Some of us are prone to it. We're made that way. But there are ways around it, and it's up to us to figure out those ways."

"Just breathe, huh?"

"Just breathe." He stood. "Come on, I'm grabbing dinner to go at the diner. I'll give you a ride home." He'd get dinner for Tyrell and his mother, too.

Later, when Mike got home and grabbed his mail, one letter stood out among the bills and advertising flyers. When he recognized the handwriting, a cold chill ran down his back. Suddenly not hungry, he put his take-out container in the refrigerator.

He wanted to throw the letter away unopened, but his curiosity got the better of him, and he opened it.

Mike's stomach twisted. He read the first sentence.

Son, I'm out now.

He dropped the letter like it was a hot potato. All the good feelings he'd had working with

Tyrell went away, and he was ten again, calling 9-1-1 while his father raged.

Needing to know where his father was now, he picked up the letter, holding it by two fingers as if it were poison. He read on, not believing what he saw. His father had become a Christian in prison? He wanted to come and see Mike?

Mike crumpled the letter and threw it hard into the nearby trash can. His father could say he'd found his faith, but that seemed like way too easy of an out for what he'd done.

Some things couldn't be forgiven.

He banged around the kitchen, then picked at the meal he'd brought home, trying to force the thoughts of his father out of his head.

Trying to keep busy, he pulled out his computer. He had a file full of papers to grade. He also had to go back to the high school later to meet with the two men he'd just hired as assistant coaches.

He felt overwhelmed. Overwhelmed and alone.

As if on cue, he noticed the lights next door turning on. Kayla and Emma were home.

He wished more than anything that he could go over there, play with his daughter, talk to Kayla. Tell her about Tyrell and about the letter. Ask her about her day.

He longed for a family. He could admit that. But he couldn't have one because of his father. He kicked the trash can where he'd thrown the letter. Pounded his hand down on the counter.

"Breathe," he reminded himself. He took deep breaths in, held, let them out, held.

Maybe he'd sounded like he had all the answers when he'd talked to Tyrell, but he didn't.

He was just trying to live his life one day at a time. And not doing a very good job of it.

Chapter Thirteen

The moment Mike walked in the door with Emma late Thursday afternoon, Kayla realized her mistake.

Mike had texted her that he wanted to pick Emma up from day care. That was helpful, allowing Kayla to get home and start dinner. But of course, he brought Emma inside; he couldn't very well drop off a two-year-old and leave her to toddle into the house by herself.

Once they were both inside, though, Emma wanted Mike to stay. "Daddy, play with Mittens," she begged.

He glanced over at Kayla, and she shrugged. She didn't want to be the bad guy and say, "No, go home, we don't want you here." Or rather, "I don't want you here," because Emma definitely wanted him to stick around.

It only took a moment for him to agree. Kayla couldn't really blame him. He wanted to spend time with his daughter, wanted to get to know her. His house wasn't yet set up for Emma to stay there, so the best place for them to get better acquainted was right there...in the home of the woman he didn't want a relationship with. And who consequently didn't want to be around him.

Kayla banged pans and slammed cupboard doors as she pulled the macaroni and cheese out of the oven and put together a salad to go with it.

"You stay dinner, Daddy," Emma said.

Kayla opened her mouth to protest and then closed it again. Of course, Mike could stay if he wanted to. No good Texas hostess would turn a guest away from her dinner table.

"No, sweetheart." He gently disentangled her arms from around his legs. "I have to go home."

Emma let out a piercing, high-pitched scream, then started to sob and gasp for breath. Her face was flushed bright red, with tears streaking down her chubby cheeks. She collapsed dramatically onto the floor, her limbs flailing, her fists pounding Mike's legs and feet.

"Emma, stop." Kayla sighed as she set the table. She could have done without the meltdown, but this was typical after a long day at day care.

Mike stared at Emma as if she were an alien. Then he glanced up at Kayla, his brow wrinkled.

"Just step away from her," Kayla said. "She'll settle down if you—"

"Okay, okay," he said at the same moment. "I'll stay."

Kayla's eyes widened and she shook her head as Emma stopped fussing and smiled. They were going to have to have a serious talk about discipline. "I was going to say ignore her. She shouldn't get what she wants by having a tantrum."

"Oh, right. Sorry." He knelt in front of his daughter. "I'll stay this time, Emma," he said, "but only if you stop whining and crying. No more bad behavior."

"Okay," Emma said. Whether she was just pleased she got her way or actually intimidated by his deep, firm voice, Kayla wasn't sure. But it was a done deal now, so she'd try to make the best of it. After she put an extra place setting at the table, they sat down together for dinner.

Mike offered to say grace and did so with eloquence, but it didn't impress Kayla. Sure, he claimed to have found faith. But he wasn't able to be in a relationship, and he didn't mind hurting Kayla over and over again. That didn't seem very Christian to her.

"Daddy pray a long time," Emma said as she watched Kayla scoop macaroni onto her plate, then pass the dish to Mike.

"He did," Kayla said with a fake smile. "Of course, the Bible has something to say about long prayers." She shot Mike a snarky glance.

He gave her a look. "I told you I'm sorry about giving in to her tantrum," he said. "And I'm sorry if I prayed too long. I'll try to be more concise next time."

If there is a next time.

Emma looked from Mike to Kayla and back again. "Why sad, Daddy and Mommy?"

"I'm still learning how to be a good daddy, Emmy Lou."

"It's been a long day. We're all tired," Kayla said.

"You good, Daddy." Emma patted his arm. "It's okay."

That little bit of sweetness melted both of them, and they smiled at each other.

Things continued to get friendlier as they ate, and Kayla realized they'd all been hungry, not just Emma. Mike complimented the food, and Emma sang songs that she'd learned in daycare, and it was actually kind of cheerful.

"Can you come to my birthday party, Daddy?" Emma asked.

"When is your birthday?" Mike asked, glancing at Kayla.

"Coming soon!" Emma crowed. A two-year-old couldn't remember dates yet, so Emma was using the answer Kayla often gave her when she asked about a future fun event.

Sorrow washed over Kayla like a waterfall. Emma's first and second birthdays had passed without Mike being there. They'd all lost out, and it was sad.

"Kayla?" He was looking at her, head tilted to one side.

"Next week, and we'll talk about it later," she said. "It's a small party. Three girls for a three-year-old."

"Sure." Mike started asking Emma questions about what she liked to do on the weekends. He was clearly distressed about everything that he didn't know about his daughter, but Kayla had to give him credit; he was trying hard to catch up.

So she invited him to read Emma her bedtime story. He followed them upstairs, and waited while Kayla helped Emma into her pajamas and brush her teeth. Then Emma showed him her current favorite storybook, focused on a giraffe at the zoo, and they settled down together. Mike tucked the covers around Emma, then sat on the side of the bed and opened the book as Kayla dimmed the light and stepped back into the shadows. She didn't want to interfere, but she hated to go downstairs before Emma nodded off.

Mike read to her, changing his voice to match the characters in the story. Emma giggled in reaction, often at first, then less and less until her eyes fluttered closed. Mike read another page and then closed the book. He stroked a stray curl back from Emma's face with a tenderness that said everything about how he felt, and Kayla quietly backed out of the room.

When they headed downstairs, Mike started to put on his jacket to leave, but turned to her. "You sounded upset after I said grace," he said. "What was that about?"

She shrugged, not looking at him, rearranging the vases of dried grasses on the mantel. "It's just strange that you're religious now, but you can't be in a relationship. It doesn't make sense to me."

"It's my faith that keeps me away," he said. "I need to do the right thing."

"What kind of faith pushes people away?"

"It's the same reason I don't see my father," he said.

"So your faith keeps you apart from people?"

"Certain people, yes," he said.

She couldn't handle hearing why she was

one of those he'd chosen to keep at a distance. "Why your dad?" she asked.

He studied her for a long moment, his coat half on. "Do you wanna hear a story?" he asked.

Just as Mike needed to learn all about Emma, Kayla needed to learn more about him, to understand him in a different way from when they'd shared fun times in Austin. "Sit down," she said. "Let me get us some tea, and then yes, I want to hear your story."

Once he was settled in a chair with a cup of tea, he began. "It's nothing you haven't heard before from some of our students," he said. "I grew up with my mom and dad fighting a lot. Lots of bruises, sometimes broken bones. But when I was ten..." His voice trailed off.

If Mike was having a hard time telling the story, this might be a bigger deal than she'd realized. "What happened when you were ten?" she asked quietly.

He sat forward, leaning his elbows on his knees, and looked at the floor. "They were having a fight as usual," he said. "And I was hiding in my bedroom as usual, trying to stay out of it."

He glanced up at her, and although the man was far from a child, a vulnerable expression revealed a glimpse of the boy he'd once been.

"I heard a weird thump, and the door slammed, and then it was totally quiet." He swallowed hard. "They were never quiet, so I went in, and my mom was on the floor."

She braced herself for whatever was coming next.

"I tried to wake up my mom, but I couldn't. I called 9-1-1, and the ambulance came, and then the police. But they couldn't wake her up, either."

Kayla could barely comprehend it. "She was... dead?"

"Yeah." He paused. "It's like a movie with scenes missing when I think about it. Which isn't very often. I remember the flashing lights, and the crime scene tape. I wanted to stay with her, but they wouldn't let me. They asked me questions about what had happened, then they went out and found my dad. Pretty quickly, I think."

"Oh, Mike." Her heart ached for the boy he'd been. What an awful memory to have to live with.

"He caused her death, is the way I try to think of it. Mom and Dad went back and forth a lot, and they were very physical with each other. She got knocked into something, and that may have been the ultimate reason she died. He maintained he didn't mean to do it. He was convicted for aggravated manslaughter, not first-degree murder."

Kayla knelt in front of him and took his hands. "Oh, Mike, I'm so sorry." She paused, then added, "You were so brave to get through that. A lot of kids would've fallen apart."

He squeezed her hands briefly, one corner of his mouth turning up in a half smile. "Oh, I definitely fell apart. Caused a lot of trouble in my teenage years, until I landed in a strict foster family. And found football."

"You've made something of yourself. You graduated high school, went to college, and became a professional football player. Think how many survivors of what you went through wouldn't have been able to do that." In fact, based on the child development courses she'd taken, the odds against that type of success for a traumatized kid were pretty high.

"I guess so," he said, sounding like he didn't believe it.

"And now you're helping kids, teaching and coaching them. Your past must be why you have such a knack with the kids who are struggling." Still holding his hands, she looked up at him, marveling. "I'm even more impressed with you than I was before."

"Thanks." He squeezed her hands again, looking thoughtful, then gently pulled his own hands away. "He wants to see me."

"Who, your dad? He wants you to come to the prison?"

"No." He shook his head. "He just got out. Wrote me a letter."

Kayla stared at him, chilled by his words. "Is he going to come here?"

"Not if I can help it." He hesitated, then added, "He says he's become a Christian and he wants to make it up to me."

His tone was curiously flat, and she tried to discern the attitude behind it. "What are you going to do? Do you believe him?"

"I don't know yet." He shook his head quickly, like a dog shaking off water. "Anyway. I appreciate your kind words, but I still can't be in a relationship with you, with anyone. I'm my father's son. I get too angry."

Outside, a neighbor's dog started barking. Moonlight filtered through the gauze curtains, illuminating the troubled lines of Mike's face. Just as his words illuminated why he'd backed off from her, not once but twice.

"No, Mike, it's not the same. You may get angry, but I've never been afraid of you, not once. I would leave Emma alone with you in a heartbeat."

"You haven't seen that side of me." He stared at the floor. "I don't trust myself. I get ugly in relationships...possessive. Remember when I saw you with your friend back in Austin? I got incredibly angry. I thought you were cheating on me."

"I told you, he was just a friend." She paused. "Is that why you broke up with me?"

He nodded once. "Not because you had a male friend. Because of my reaction to it. I scared myself. I came really close to getting out of control."

"But you didn't." Her heart was full and confused. "I feel like you're too hard on yourself. You're not a bad guy, Mike."

He touched her face, lightly, gently. Then he stood. "I should go. But I just want you to know, Kayla, if things were different, I would want to be with you." His gaze lingered on her for a moment. Then he walked out the door.

Kayla sank down into a chair, feeling too tired to support herself. Hearing his story made her heart ache for him. And he seemed to have reached an awful conclusion about himself. Unless he could overcome this—this fear about his own nature—things could never work between them.

Talking, reassuring him, wasn't going to fix

it. She could see that. But she was too tired to figure out if there was another solution, and what it might be. Didn't know if she should push it. Did she want to help this troubled man overcome his past? Would it cause him to stick around for his daughter and for her…or to bolt?

As she was getting ready for bed, she heard a banging noise outside. She looked out the window and saw a shadow running through the yard.

Someone was out there. Her heart rate accelerated.

Mike's revelation flashed through her mind, and panic rose in her.

His father had written him a letter. That meant the man knew his address. Had he come back to cause Mike trouble?

Chapter Fourteen

Mike puttered around his kitchen, putting things away and basking in Kayla's kind reaction to his family's horrible history.

It was something he never talked about, figuring that people would pity him, at best. More likely, people would be put off by him, the product of his sorry family.

Kayla had reacted differently. Instead of fearing him, she'd thought him brave and resilient. She'd been struck by what he'd achieved despite his background. Was she right? Had he overcome it, even done so in an impressive way?

He put away dishes and wiped down counters, musing. If she were right about him, if he'd overcome his childhood past and come out on the other side, did that mean he could move on?

His phone buzzed. When he saw Kayla's name on the lock screen, he smiled to himself. Risky business, this hope thing. But maybe... He clicked into the call.

"Look outside, between our houses," Kayla said without preamble. "I think there's someone out there."

In a flash, Mike went from happy to high alert. He turned off his light, slid his feet into shoes, and went to the window.

Several dark forms were visible between their houses, beside Kayla's garage. The way they moved reassured him, because it was what he saw in the classroom every day. "I see them," he said. "I'll take care of it. Keep this line open and call 9-1-1 if it sounds bad. But I think it's just kids."

He slipped out the door and made his way over to the bushes near the garage. Hidden there, he watched three shadowy forms moving and laughing. Definitely kids.

When the moon emerged from behind a cloud, he realized who was there and what they were doing. Anger swept through him, tensing his muscles and sharpening his senses.

Kayla's garage was a ramshackle structure, and they'd kicked in whole sections. Worse, on the garage were spray-painted words and symbols not fit for polite company.

The perpetrators were Winston Compton, the former quarterback he'd kicked off the team, and a couple of his friends.

"You still there?" he said into the phone.

"I'm here."

"No need for cops," he said. "I've got this." Shoving it back in his pocket, he marched over to them, his heart pounding loudly in his ears. "What do you think you're doing?" He pulled Winston off the wooden crate he was standing on and away from the wall.

A metal spray paint can clattered to the ground. The other boys scattered.

Anger throbbed in Mike's temples, and his hands balled into fists. "You're defacing someone's property. You need to get out of here and never come back."

Winston swaggered toward him. "You think you're something, old man?" A stream of expletives rolled off his lips, including some ugly words about Kayla.

Mike lost it. "Shut your trap," he yelled. "Get out of here! Go on, go!"

"You'll have to make me." The boy's voice was gloating. Goading. Obnoxious.

Mike raised a fist and then consciously loosened it. Stay cool. Breathe. "Do you want the police involved? Because that can happen."

Suddenly, Winston ran toward Mike and headbutted him.

Mike staggered back, tripped over something, crashed to the ground. He got quickly to his feet, his focus narrowing to the boy, his movements, his fighting stance.

Winston came at Mike again, and Mike lifted his hands to protect his face and neck. "Coward," Winston taunted when he realized that Mike wasn't fighting back. He landed a punch on Mike's chin.

Mike saw stars and raised his fists.

Winston ran right into one of them, hard enough that Mike's hand stung. The boy let out a howl, holding a hand to his face. "You hit me!" he yelled, running at Mike again.

From the corner of his eye, Mike saw Kayla's door open.

No way was he letting this kid get to Kayla. He grabbed Winston by the collar of his coat and his belt, carried him off the property, and dropped him onto the grassy median of the road. "Get out of here and don't come back."

"You'll be sorry!" Winston ran after the other boys.

Mike's breath came fast. He hadn't been this angry in…well, maybe never. He was also confused. He hadn't hit Winston, and yet the kid had said he'd be sorry. But Winston had hit him and run into him.

Dimly, he heard Kayla's voice. "Mike, are you okay? Should I call the cops?"

"Get inside, I'm fine," Mike said as the adrenaline left his body. Replacing it was a dull shame.

Winston had gotten hurt. No matter how much the kid deserved punishment, Mike didn't want to be the person who could injure a teenager. Didn't want to be the guy whose anger escalated from one to ten in a heartbeat.

But that was who he was.

Moving slowly, he got a big bed sheet from his house and nailed it over the offensive words and images. He didn't want Kayla or Emma seeing them, didn't want anyone else in town to see them, either. But even through his heartache and confusion, he knew he needed to leave this evidence here in case Kayla wanted to get the police involved.

A flashlight bobbed toward him. Kayla. She shone it toward his feet, then flashed it over the rest of him. Her mouth dropped open and her forehead creased. "You're hurt."

That was when he saw a trickle of blood on his hand, and more from an abrasion on his forearm. When had he fallen? "I'm okay," he said, wiping his hand on his jeans. "Go inside. They could come back, so lock the doors."

"Come over, and I'll help you get cleaned up," she said. "Was it Winston?"

"Yes, and he did some damage to your garage. You might want to report it tomorrow."

"I'm not going to report a kid for a little spray-painting," she said. "You, on the other hand, got injured. Come on." She took his hand gently and tugged him toward her house.

He followed reluctantly. "I'll be fine. You need your rest."

"Don't be silly. We need to get you cleaned up and then figure out what to do about those boys."

Mike barely listened. Now that the immediate situation was settled, he felt like a fool. Why hadn't he just called the police, let them take care of it? Why had he taken matters into his own hands?

Because you're your father's son, came the voice in his head.

He'd seen the expression on Kayla's face— fear and horror. He knew it well because it was an expression he'd worn often as a kid.

This time, though, he was the cause of it. He was the perpetrator. It was what he'd always feared about himself, and now, here it was, coming true.

Kayla led Mike into the house and directed him to a kitchen chair. She'd been afraid, but now she felt so, so warm. She had to admit it was awesome to have a man who wanted to take care of her and protect her.

She found a washcloth and used it to carefully wipe the dirt from Mike's bruised face. When she saw that his arm had a gravel burn, she went to the refrigerator, pulled out an ice pack from the freezer, and handed it to him. "Hold this to your chin," she said. Then she sat down next to him.

He hadn't said anything yet. But that had to have been a disturbing fight with one of his students. She wasn't surprised he needed to process it silently.

As she carefully cleaned his arm, she thought about what had changed. A short time ago, she wouldn't have accepted any man's protectiveness. But now here she was, appreciating it from Mike. Could she possibly be growing? Learning to accept help from others?

Mike winced when she wiped off a particularly bad section of his arm. To distract him, she said, "I can't believe they came over and did that. I mean, I get why Winston is mad at you. You kicked him off the team. But why is he mad at me?"

"Because of your connection to me," he said. They were the first words he'd spoken since he'd walked in the house, and his voice was dull.

She went to the sink, rinsed out her cloth, and grabbed some antibiotic ointment. She brought the supplies back over and went to work. "One way or another, we need to take care of this. You may not know this, but we could do it informally. We could have someone from the school, or even my dad, talk to his parents. Make it clear that this kind of behavior will go to the police next time. Or we could do it right now through the law. What do you think?"

He shook his head. "Doesn't make a difference," he said.

She dabbed antibiotic on to his injury, trying to be gentle. "You're pretty upset, aren't you?"

"I'm not happy with what happened, of course. And I'm even less happy with how I reacted."

"You protected me and Emma, Mike. You did a good thing."

He shook his head. "Unnecessary roughness."

"I was looking out the window. I saw that he attacked you. It didn't look like you hit him at all."

"Doesn't matter. I shouldn't have touched him. I'm the adult."

Kayla didn't like how he was reacting to the situation. Where was the Mike she had been starting to know? Who was this sad, self-loathing man in front of her?

She finished cleaning his arm. Then she got a couple of large bandages to cover the wound. When she pulled the ice pack away from his chin, holding on to his hand, she looked at his face. "You're going to have a nice big bruise."

He shrugged.

"Tell me what's wrong, Mike. Why are you so quiet about everything?"

"Disappointed in myself."

"I'm not," she said. "I'm proud of you."

His phone buzzed, and he pulled it out of his back pocket. Kayla could hear an angry man's voice, though she couldn't recognize the words.

"Yes, sir," Mike said quietly. "Yes, we've discussed this." He listened for another moment. "Yes, that's correct."

He listened to what was obviously a tirade for a little bit longer.

"Did you ask your son what he was doing on Miss Stewart's property?"

More shouting from the other end of the line.

"I understand," Mike said. He hadn't looked at Kayla during the whole conversation, and he didn't look at her now as he ended the call.

"What is it?" She pulled her chair to where she could see his face better.

"Winston's father is taking me to court. Pressing charges."

"For what?" Kayla asked. She tried not to think about how much power Winston's family had in this town.

"Apparently, Winston has a broken tooth and some bruising on his face."

Her heart sank, even as protective feelings rose in her. "Not from what you did. He may have fallen down, and he definitely hit you, but you didn't hit him or push him."

"Thank you, Kayla. Thanks for everything. Go get some rest."

He stood and turned toward the door. She got up quickly, wanting to hug him, to thank him. But realizing her intent, he quickened his pace and was gone.

That had been strange. And Kayla didn't know what to do.

She could follow him, push him, try to force him to explain what was going on in his head.

She had tried that while she was cleaning him up, and he hadn't responded.

Should she leave him alone? Maybe he was the type of person who needed to process difficult things on his own.

She wasn't sure that was good for him. It seemed likely to make him spiral down into a darkness that had its roots in his difficult childhood.

And processing things in a solitary way wasn't good for any relationship they were going to have, even if they were just going to be co-parents. They needed to be able to talk to each other. She needed to feel free to go to him. He needed to listen to her and respond.

On the other hand, she didn't want to overstep. Her experience with the type of trauma he'd faced was limited, almost nonexistent. Moreover, she felt so warmly toward him, she didn't want to accidentally push him away.

Men and women processed things differently. Most women needed to talk the problems out. Men, like Mike—especially those who'd been involved in a hypermasculine world like football—had almost certainly learned to repress their feelings.

She'd try to sleep tonight and see where things stood in the morning.

Chapter Fifteen

On Saturday morning, Mike guzzled down coffee. His eyes felt grainy and his muscles ached—not so much from the squabble with the boys as from the tension.

He had to get out of here.

That was the conclusion he'd come to after tossing and turning all night. He had nearly lost control. Being so close to hurting a child had showed him that he was capable of violence.

He didn't belong in a town like this, in a position of authority. He didn't deserve to be a father to Emma nor as a partner to Kayla.

He ran his fingers through his hair and then let his head sink into his hands, elbows on the kitchen table. He needed to get out of range of his bad emotions. He heard the sound of children's voices outside and was immediately drawn to the window. Emma and Kayla were over in the neighbor's yard. It looked like they were introducing the kittens to each other.

There was lots of talk and laughter, especially from the girls.

They have a support system here, he reminded himself. Emma and Kayla would be fine without him. They'd be even better once he was gone.

He went down to the basement and found the boxes he'd broken down and stacked when he'd moved in. He carried them upstairs and started building them with packing tape, his throat tight.

Just keep moving, he told himself.

Starting in his bedroom, he began packing up clothes and shoes. Then he moved to the kitchen and stacked the few kitchen supplies he had brought with him on the counter.

He went to the refrigerator, planning to box up some food, but a picture hung with a magnet on the door caught his eye.

It was a picture that Emma had made for him at day care—a messy pink handprint. On it, her teacher had written "To Daddy, from Emma."

He swallowed hard. That was precious. He went to his study and got a file folder to put it into and keep it protected. He set it carefully in the kitchen box. It would go up on the refrigerator of wherever he landed next, if he could bear it.

He was almost done packing when there was a pounding on the door. His heart jumped a little as he went to answer it, but it wasn't Kayla. Nor was it William Compton's father or his lawyer. It was Tyrell and a couple of kids from the team.

"Hey, guys," Mike said. "You're up early on a Saturday."

"You look bad," Tyrell said, frowning as he studied Mike's face and bandages. "Compton's going around saying he ran you out of town and he's back in as quarterback."

"Not exactly, but... I am leaving."

"Why?" Betrayal was written on Tyrell's face.

"It's personal," he said. "Give me a hand here, will you?" He indicated the stack of boxes he'd put beside the door.

They were good kids, and they did what he said. They moved boxes for him, stacking them in his truck, and then stuck around to help him pack up the rest of his kitchen supplies. He ended up giving each of them a bag of food to take home. Not much space for that in a motel room.

"You shouldn't go, man," Tyrell said. He flung a stack of dish towels into the box. "We were going to have a good team this year.

You've been better to me than anyone else has been in a long time."

"You can keep doing well, Tyrell," Mike said. "You're a great kid and a great player."

Tyrell made a disgusted sound in his throat. "Nobody wants to stick around," he muttered.

The boys carried boxes out to the truck, none of them smiling or joking around as was their usual habit. Mike felt guilty. Awful. He was letting these boys down.

His phone buzzed, and he stepped into his bedroom to take the call. It was the principal, Ron Garcia.

"What's this about a lawsuit?" Garcia asked.

Mike explained what had happened last night. Garcia had him go over it again.

"I think I've got it," the principal said finally. "Sit tight. I'll make some calls."

"No need to stick your neck out," Mike said. "It's fine. I'm thinking through what to do."

In reality, he had already decided that he needed to leave Tumbleweed. But he didn't want to say it until he called around to help find a replacement for himself, at least as a coach, and hopefully as a teacher, too.

He was sad about leaving. But when you were a violent, angry person—a danger to others—you had to take precautions. If you didn't, disaster could lie ahead.

"We gonna see you on Monday?" Tyrell asked after the last box had been loaded.

"Yes. I'll talk with the team then."

The boys climbed into their car and drove off, their disappointed expressions staying with Mike.

"Hey, Mike," came a hesitant voice behind him.

Kayla.

He turned to face her. She had Emma by the hand.

Kayla looked from Mike to the truck. Then she looked at Mike again. "What's going on?"

"I'm moving back to the motel," he said. It was a stopgap measure while he figured out what to do next.

"Why?" She didn't look surprised, exactly. She just looked sad.

"I'm not good working with kids or being around them," he said. "Including my own."

She stared at him, raw pain in her eyes. "You're moving away from here, or from Tumbleweed?"

He paused. "Both," he said finally.

Emma pulled away from Kayla and ran over to her sandbox.

"Don't do it, Mike!" Kayla marched over to the truck and tried to pull one of the boxes out. It was a heavy one, too heavy for her, and he walked over and put a hand on it to stop her.

"It's for the best," he said, shoving the box back into place.

"In what universe is it for the best for you to abandon your daughter?"

The words hung in the air, pressing on him, slicing into his heart.

"You don't know what I'm capable of, Kayla, but I do," he said. "Believe me, it's for the best if I leave."

"Daddy, go bye-bye?" Emma had run back over, and she stood before him, looking up with trust in her eyes.

"That's right," he said through a tight throat.

"You don't have to do this," Kayla said. "This is your past talking."

He stepped away. "I'm out of here," he said, looking away from her emotional eyes.

Emma jumped and reached for him, and he couldn't help it. He picked her up and swung her high one more time.

He covered her with kisses until she giggled, and called her Emmy Lou. Then he set her down beside Kayla.

"See you later, Daddy," she said, waving.

He couldn't speak. He just nodded and strode to his truck and climbed in.

Emma ran over to where she could see him and waved harder. "Back soon, Daddy," she said.

Mike looked at Kayla. In her eyes, there was an understanding that he wouldn't come back.

He made sure that Kayla had Emma by the hand, then he drove off in a blur of tears.

Somehow, Kayla managed to get herself and Emma to church the next day, partly because she wanted Emma to have the chance to play with the nursery kids, who were definitely going to be more cheerful companions than Kayla was.

Mostly because she needed to pray her way into forgetting about Mike Cook forever.

He had fulfilled her worst expectations. He had moved away abruptly. True, she had his forwarding address for the moment. She knew he was planning to stay at the motel. But he'd also said he was leaving Tumbleweed. Leaving both Kayla and his daughter this time.

Unbelievable.

She had intended all along to be strong and independent for Emma's sake. The hurt she felt now suggested independence had been the right goal.

But another voice nagged at her. Mike was

good for Emma. Mike was good for the kids at the school.

When he was being his confident self, Mike was very, very good for Kayla.

He was leaving her again.

But now she understood why.

Mike's childhood experiences had been awful. She got that now. And they'd left deep scars in him. That much was obvious.

She sat through the service, and the prayers and scriptures washed over her, sinking in, providing comfort. She was a child of God. God valued her. She knew it, and the church service reminded her of it. So the idea of being left by a man didn't make her feel totally insecure, totally worthless.

Just very, very sad.

If Mike couldn't get past the things that had happened to him, then he couldn't be there for Kayla.

Okay, she could accept that. She was miserable about it, but she could accept that.

But what about Emma?

In the press of the crowd after church, she noticed people standing in clusters, talking with an intensity that suggested something had happened. Many were looking in the same direction.

What were they looking at?

A tall figure at the back of the church.

Mike.

They were looking at Mike. And a few of them glanced at her as well.

Mike was obviously trying to get out the door. He'd sat in the back, probably wanting to leave without being noticed, but Mike was impossible to ignore. People crowded around him, blocking him from leaving. She could tell by the way he rubbed the back of his neck that he was uncomfortable, but he was speaking to everyone, obviously trying to be civil.

From people's reactions, she was guessing that word of Mike's supposed attack on Winston had gotten out, probably from Winston's family.

She read the sleepless night he'd had in the dark circles under his eyes, the stress in the tight line of his jaw. Bad enough that he was reliving his past and trying to leave the child and the job he loved so much, but he was also facing intense small-town Texas gossip.

Maybe this was the first time he'd experienced that? But no, he'd mentioned something about how notorious his parents had been. That meant the gossip could be plunging him further into the past.

Kayla knew she should be strong. Wash her

hands of him and forget him. That was what a truly strong woman would do.

But she couldn't help but feel compassion for the father of her child.

Across the sanctuary, she saw Patty Wright talking intently to her father. Her finger poked into his chest as she scolded him. She kept glancing over in Mike's direction. What was that about?

"Hey, girl," came a familiar voice behind her. Kayla turned and saw her neighbor, Shanae. It was a relief to see her friendly face.

Shanae tilted her head to one side, looking at her. "You okay?"

"Yeah." She nodded, trying to convince herself and failing. "Kinda."

"Maliyah was asking about Emma's birthday party," she said. "We're still invited, aren't we?"

"Of course you are. I just haven't done any planning and...wow, it's less than a week away."

"Next Saturday. But you said it's small, right?"

"Right."

Shanae studied her. "Come on, let's get you home," she said. "Even a small event takes a little bit of planning. I'll help you. Mike will be at the party, right?"

Kayla swallowed hard and shook her head. "I don't think so," she rasped out.

The thought of the party without Mike there made Kayla's tears overflow.

Shanae insisted on following her home to make sure she and Emma were safe. In the kitchen, she ordered Kayla into a chair.

"Why don't you girls go play dolls?" she said to Maliyah and Emma.

"Mommy, play with us," Maliyah suggested.

"Nope," Shanae said. "Go play, girls." Her voice brooked no nonsense, and the girls got wide-eyed and hurried out of the room.

Shanae made herself at home, fixing them both cups of tea. The kitten jumped into Kayla's lap, and she petted it as it arched against her hand, purring.

"Now, tell me what happened." Shanae pulled out a chair across from Kayla.

So Kayla explained that Mike had moved back into the motel and was planning to leave town, that he thought he was a danger to young people, including Emma, because of major trauma in his past, and because of what had happened with Winston Compton.

"Wow." Shanae shook her head, sipped tea, and frowned.

"What do you think I should do?" Kayla asked.

"At the moment? I'd say withhold judgment.

He's Emma's dad, and you want him to continue to act as a dad, if possible."

"He doesn't want to be a dad," Kayla said.

"He adores that girl. You know he does."

"You're right." Kayla thought of the expression on Mike's face as he said goodbye to Emma. "But is that enough to overcome how much he hates himself?"

"Only with God's help," Shanae said. "But our God is mighty."

"Mighty enough to fix something this big?" Kayla knew she was supposed to think so, but she was having trouble believing it.

"He brought the man here after you thought you'd never see him again. Moved him in right next door, and you know that was a God thing. He's been a blessing to so many of the boys on that team. To you and Emma, too. If He could do all that, He can fix Mike inside as well."

Kayla wanted to believe that. Oh, how she wanted to believe it.

"He can fix you, too." Shanae was looking at her with a level, compassionate gaze. "If you want to be fixed."

Kayla closed her eyes for a moment, then opened them again. "I do want to be fixed," she said. "I want what's best for Emma. And for Mike, too." Because she couldn't hate him, no matter how bad things were right now.

"Put it into His hands, girl," Shanae said. "He is a mighty God. He'll work it all for good, according to His plan."

So they prayed together, and Kayla did her best to dump the whole situation into the hands of the Lord.

She still felt as if someone had taken a shovel and scooped out her insides. She hurt for herself, and even more, she hurt for Emma. But the sharpness of the pain was blunted. She'd felt the Lord's reassurance, like healing balm over a wound.

"Now, put it out of your mind. He's got this." Shanae stood. "Maliyah and I need to get home. Will you be okay?"

"Thanks so much, Shanae. We'll be okay," Kayla said. She didn't know how. But she knew it was true.

With God's help, everything would be all right.

Chapter Sixteen

On Tuesday around five o'clock in the afternoon, Kayla drove home, feeling decent for the first time in a few days.

Work had definitely helped get herself back together. To get herself out of bed yesterday and today, to feign cheerfulness as she dressed for school and got Emma fed and ready for day care. And to teach her classes with some degree of energy.

Even more than work, it had taken a lot of prayer. She'd come closer than ever before in her life to obeying the Apostle Paul's command to pray without ceasing. She'd prayed her way through each day and fallen asleep praying at night.

The next part of the verse from 1 Thessalonians—*In every thing give thanks*—had proven harder, but she was trying. She gave thanks for her daughter's good health, for her job, for her friends, and her father. It helped, even though her heart still ached.

In the back seat, Emma sang. The cat, Mittens, was in a crate beside her. It was a beautiful day, warm and breezy, with the setting sun casting a golden light over downtown Tumbleweed.

Emma segued into a made-up song that consisted mostly of the word *cat* repeated over and over, at different volumes and in different tones. She sounded so happy that Kayla was glad she'd picked her up early and let her come along on this preliminary veterinary visit.

Abruptly, Emma stopped singing. "Daddy!" she cried out. "I see Daddy!"

Kayla's hard-won peace of mind evaporated, and her gut clenched. Would she ever escape Mike? She'd seen him yesterday and today in school, and every time she pulled into her driveway, she was faced with his now-empty home.

"Mommy, stop! I see Daddy!"

Sure enough, there he was. He was walking along the sidewalk toward the motel. She didn't want to stop, but Emma's pleading voice and the slump of Mike's shoulders made her hit the brakes.

She thought of the prayer she had shared with Shanae, and of her friend's wise words. She'd cast her cares on Him. Was Mike's presence now a God thing?

She pulled over beside Mike and lowered the back window.

"Daddy, Daddy!" Emma bounced up and down in her car seat.

Mike stopped but didn't turn toward them. He stood utterly still, his shoulders tense. For a horrible moment, Kayla thought he was going to walk away.

Then he lifted his chin, turned, and approached the car. Without glancing at Kayla, he went directly to Emma's open window. "Hi there, Emmy Lou," he said.

"I'm Emma," she said, giggling.

The happy sound made Kayla's heart ache. This poor little girl. She'd already come to love Mike, and she was confident in his love. Was that confidence going to be shattered?

"Daddy, we took Mittens to the vet!"

He braced his hands on the car roof and leaned toward Emma, looking into the back seat. "Is she okay?"

"She's good! She weighs six pounds."

"That's great." Mike took a step back and looked at Kayla's closed window. "Hey," he said.

She lowered her window halfway. "Hey," she said.

"Everything else okay?" he asked her.

That was a loaded question if she'd ever heard one. "You mean with the cat or…"

The question hung in the air for a moment. Then Mike's jaw tightened. "The cat," he said.

Of course, he was only asking about the cat. He hadn't even wanted to see them. His innate human decency was the only thing that had made him turn toward the car and greet his daughter—not any kind of feelings about Kayla.

"The cat's fine." She tried to inject energy into her voice, but failed. "Very healthy. Got her shots."

"She got shots, Daddy!" Emma cried out from the back seat.

Cars were driving by. A couple of pedestrians looked over and waved.

Mike was looking at Kayla. He opened his mouth, then shut it again.

Oh boy. She knew him well enough to see that he was in turmoil. This wasn't easy on him, either.

"Come home with us for dinner, Daddy!" Emma leaned forward.

"I can't, sweetie." His face was a mask of misery.

"Please, please, please, please?"

As she watched him struggle with how to answer, a slideshow of the past few weeks passed through her mind. Seeing him at the teachers' meeting for the first time in three years. The moment when he'd met Emma at her house. How he'd followed his newly discovered daughter around at the park, tentatively starting to figure out the parenting thing. The easy, comfortable way they'd laughed together at the dinner table.

She thought of him explaining his horrible past to her. Going after the vandalizing boys, so protective.

Kissing her.

Telling her he was leaving her. Again.

"Sorry, sweetie," he said to Emma in a voice that was a little ragged.

"Please, Daddy! Please!" Emma started to cry.

Mike took a step back.

Kayla put the car into gear, closed the windows, and squealed away.

In the back seat, Emma sobbed.

Kayla's own eyes were blurry enough that it felt a little unsafe to even be driving. She took deep breaths, blinked to clear her eyes, and focused on the road.

They made it home safely, and pulled into the driveway. Her eyes went immediately to Mike's empty house.

Emma's cries escalated. "Ow, Mommy!"

Kayla got out of the car, wiped her eyes on

her sleeve, and opened the back door. "Come on, honey, it's okay," she said. Even though it wasn't.

"Mittens hurt me! I don't like her anymore!" Emma held out a tiny hand. Blood was beading up on a small scratch on her thumb.

"Oh, no, an ouchie." Kayla automatically spoke in her calming mom-voice as she fumbled for tissues, wiped the blood with one, and dabbed at Emma's eyes with the other. "Did you poke your fingers into the crate?"

Emma nodded. "Bad kitty," she said, her lower lip sticking out.

Kayla got Emma out of her car seat and set her feet on the ground. "Mittens was scared, and that's why she hurt you. She doesn't like riding in the car, and she didn't like the vet poking and prodding her."

Emma looked unconvinced. "Mittens, you stay out here. I don't like you." Emma turned decidedly away from the car, then peeked back over her shoulder.

Kayla pulled the crate from the back seat. "We still take care of those we love, even when we're mad at them," she said.

She took Emma's good hand, held the crate in the other, and headed inside.

Those we love.

Realization washed over her. She did love Mike. She did want to take care of him, to put a smile back on his face, despite what he had done.

But she didn't want to beg, wouldn't do it. Leaving was something he'd done to her before. She couldn't go through convincing him to come back and then losing him again. Couldn't put Emma through that.

As she turned to close the door, she saw Shanae pulling up into her driveway. The woman got out of the car, waved, and made prayer hands.

Kayla waved as she shut the door. *Okay, Shanae, I'll pray about it.*

Tuesday evening, Mike was having a late dinner at the Friendly Fork Diner when Jim Stewart burst in like an avenging sheriff in a Western, making the bells on the door rattle. He spotted Mike and marched toward his table.

Heads turned in the crowded diner, and conversation died down for a few seconds.

Mike sighed. He'd put in a long day of teaching while listening to students plead with him to stay. The football team had alternately complained and looked hurt throughout their weight training workout, which every single potential team member had attended.

Then there had been that awful encounter with Kayla and Emma. His daughter's begging him to come home to dinner had nearly broken him. Even worse had been the hurt visible in Kayla's eyes.

He felt lower than a piece of gum scraped off someone's shoe. Given Jim's expression, things weren't going to get much better.

Mike hadn't been all that hungry when he'd come in, and now his appetite deserted him entirely.

Jim slid into the seat across from him without asking. "I stopped by my daughter's house a few minutes ago," he said. "Both she and Emma were upset. Because of you."

"Yes, sir." There was no point denying it.

"I don't like people making my girls cry."

The thought that he'd made Kayla cry twisted Mike's stomach into a knot.

Jim studied him for a moment, then waved down the waitress. "I'll have one of those," he said, pointing to Mike's burger and fries platter.

"You don't have to hang around," Mike said. "I'm leaving."

"You're not done eating," Jim said, gesturing toward Mike's almost-full plate.

"I mean, I'm leaving town."

He waited for pleasure to cross Jim's face, but

it didn't happen. Instead, Jim shook his head. "That's what I want to talk to you about," he said.

Of course, it figured that Jim had already heard. He was the former mayor, not the current one, but no doubt everyone still told him everything. If he hadn't heard it on the gossip circuit, then Kayla must have told him.

Mike prepared himself for a lecture. It couldn't be any harsher than what he'd been saying to himself ever since he'd acted so deplorably toward Winston Compton and his cronies.

But the lecture didn't come. "I spoke with Patty Wright," Jim said. "You've met her, I think."

Mike nodded.

A dark flush crossed Jim's weathered face. "She gave me a pretty big scolding."

Despite his misery, curiosity flickered in Mike. "She scolded you? What for?"

"She heard how I threatened to get you fired after finding out you were Emma's dad," he said. "Thought I'd been too hard on you. Didn't want you to leave, and, well, I've come to agree with her."

Mike thought he must've misheard Jim. "What?"

"I'm asking you to stay in Tumbleweed and be involved in Kayla and Emma's life," Jim said.

The voices around them, the clatter of dishes and silverware, the cheesy music from the old-fashioned jukebox, all faded from Mike's awareness in the shock of what Jim was saying.

The waitress came over, refilled Mike's coffee, and poured a cup for Jim.

"Why would you want me involved in their lives?" Mike asked, genuinely confused. "Don't you know what I did?"

"I know exactly what you did," Jim said. "You kicked some troublemaker kids off Kayla's property. You protected my daughter and granddaughter, and I appreciate that. And I like that you took care of the team by booting Winston Compton off it in the first place."

"That's not the way Compton's family sees it."

"It's the truth. I have proof."

"Wait a minute, wait a minute," Mike said. "What do you mean, you have proof?"

Jim leaned back and stretched out his legs, his booted feet crossing in the aisle. "Because I watched the footage from Kayla's porch camera," Jim said.

Mike stared blankly. "Kayla has a porch camera?"

Again, Jim's face colored. "She doesn't know it," he said. "I had one installed for her protection. The feed comes to my house."

Mike put aside the invasion of Kayla's privacy to think about later. He knew Jim had his daughter's best interests at heart, even if he was overbearing about it. "And you saw what happened? What did you see?"

"I saw young Compton try to set you up," Jim said. "He made it look like you hit him, but you didn't. He ran himself into your fist and cried wolf. I have no respect for that."

Mike just stared at him, speechless.

But Jim wasn't done yet. "You've become a solid member of this community in just a short while," he said. "You're a good coach, and most importantly, you're a loving and responsible father."

"I'm glad you think so," Mike said, trying to process the praise. "But meanwhile, Winston Compton's folks are filing charges against me."

Jim let out a dry laugh. "The Compton family are a bunch of troublemakers. Troublemakers with money, which is the worst kind. But that lawsuit will go nowhere."

"I've been told he's pretty powerful in this town," Mike said.

"Not as powerful as I am," Jim said bluntly.

"I'd like to offer you the services of the Stewart family lawyer."

"You want me to stay, even knowing what you know? That Kayla has suffered because of me?"

"I know my daughter," he said. "She still cares for you, if you haven't messed that up."

Mike felt a slight lifting of his spirits, but there was more blocking his ability to take what Jim was offering. "You may not know this, but I come from bad blood," he said. "My father spent time in prison for—"

Jim waved a hand. "I know what he did. Don't you think I had you investigated before offering you this job, and even more when I found out your connection to Kayla and Emma?"

Mike stared at him. "You know about my parents?" And yet the man had pushed for him to get the coaching job, had invited him into his home?

"I do," Jim said, his eyes crinkling with sympathy. "And I also know it's not your fault what your parents did. You can overcome it. In fact, I hope you will." He stood. "My lawyer will give you a call. He should be able to make the Compton lawsuit go away."

Mike was still shocked. "But why are you doing this for me?"

"Your team came to me asking for help to keep you as coach," he said. "Kids are astute. If those boys have come to respect you in the short time you've been here, you're on a good path."

Mike was touched to think of the boys going to Jim Stewart.

Jim waved down the waitress again. "Box my meal up," he said. Then he turned back to Mike. "Kayla is another story. You're gonna have to do something to convince her you won't run off again. I'll leave you to think about that." He plucked Mike's check off the table, handed it and a fifty-dollar bill to the waitress, took his boxed meal, and walked out.

The man knew how to get things done, that was for sure. Mike was stunned, but the hope inside him was growing.

Now all he had to do was think of how to make things up to Kayla.

Chapter Seventeen

"Up there, there's still a streak." Mike stood with his arms crossed, studying the side of the garage that Winston and his friends had vandalized.

It was Saturday afternoon. Five members of the football team had come with him to help repair the damage, and Mike felt like he was repairing relationships with them, too. No one was asking him if he still planned to leave, but they kept giving him side-glances. He had heard them talking amongst themselves. They wanted him to stay.

He wanted to stay, too.

The garage was now painted bright white and looked a lot better. They hadn't been able to repair the structural damage to one corner of the garage, but at least they'd made a big improvement. Most importantly, the offensive graffiti was completely gone. Whether this would help his cause, he didn't know. But he wanted to ingratiate himself to Kayla, to make it up to her for what he'd done.

He was still confused and in turmoil. He wanted to be a good father but doubted his own ability to not live out his family's genetic tendencies toward violence. He'd been talking to Pastor Rob about it. The guy was just a little older than Mike, but he'd been through some things in his life and he was a good listener. He'd also let Mike know where to find more counseling locally if he wanted it. Mike was seriously considering it.

Even though he doubted himself, he had realized, when Emma and Kayla had stopped the car by him, that he was hurting Emma by staying away. Maybe, for her sake and with some hard work, he could stop letting the past derail his future.

"Almost done, guys," he said. "Let's start cleaning up."

As he was gathering up the paintbrushes to clean them, a car pulled up in front of Kayla's house. Then another. From each car, a little girl with a gift emerged, rushing into Kayla's house while a mom and a dad trailed behind them.

They were dressed up so cute, and those presents...

Today was Emma's birthday. He knew that

and was planning to shop for a gift after they finished here.

But he'd forgotten about Emma's birthday party. He hadn't been invited, at least not by Kayla.

He understood why. He'd angered Kayla terribly on multiple occasions, including that last moment when she had driven a sobbing Emma away. He had no right to go to his daughter's birthday party, but it still hurt.

"Hey, thanks for doing that," said the neighbor from across the street.

"Sure thing," Mike said, pulling himself together. "Shanae, right?"

"That's right, and this is my daughter, Maliyah."

"Can I go up to the door?" Maliyah asked. "Can I, Mom?"

"Sure, I'll be right there," Shanae said. She looked at Mike. "Guess you're not coming in?"

"Nope. Not invited."

Shanae's eyes creased in sympathy. "Keep trying, Mike. Kayla knows about forgiveness. She'll get there."

"I hope so."

"I promised her I'd help with the party. I better go in." Shanae looked over his shoulder behind him. "Hey, looks like someone wants to see you." She waved and walked off.

Mike turned and saw an old man standing on the street, looking at him.

He was a broad-shouldered man who would have looked tall if he weren't hunched over. His clothes were ragged. And he was staring at Mike.

All the breath whooshed out of Mike's chest as he saw, for the first time in almost twenty years, his father.

A tornado of emotions swirled inside him. The last time he'd seen the man had been through a kitchen window, running away after Mike's mother had fallen to the floor. But Mike also remembered that he'd loved his dad once, that his father had taken him fishing, and had helped him build a soapbox car that had beat every other kid's car at the school.

"Is that all, Coach?" Tyrell came over to him. He, and all the boys, looked from Mike to his father.

"That's all, Tyrell, thanks. You guys did good. Thanks again." His throat tightened on the last words.

He waited until Tyrell had followed the other boys away and then walked over to his father.

Up close, Mike could see that his assessment

was correct: The man had aged, and not well. His face was deeply lined, and he wore one arm in a sling that looked permanent.

"What are you doing here?" Mike asked.

"I've come to try to make amends. Been stopping by last couple days, knocking on your door. Got no answer."

"I don't live there anymore." They were standing six feet apart. "And I don't want you to make amends. There's no way you can."

"Understood." His dad's voice was familiar, except Mike had never heard that quiet, humble tone before.

The street was empty, aside from the boys' car disappearing into the distance. In a neighbor's yard, a dog barked.

His father cleared his throat. "It's not forgivable, what I did. I never meant to take your mother's life, but I did mean to hurt her, and that was wrong. I know that now."

Mike crossed his arms over his chest.

"I've changed," Mike's father said. "I'm a new creation, but I don't expect you to want to have anything to do with me. I just wanted to tell you to your face that I'm sorry and see if there's anything I can do for you."

"There's nothing." Mike's feelings swirled and roiled inside him. He felt a little sick.

"Like maybe help you with the smashed-in corner of that garage?" His father took a step toward Kayla's garage and tilted his head to one side, studying it.

Oh, yeah. In the midst of all his father's weaknesses, there was one strength: Dad had been good at fixing things. That had been his line of work, when he'd actually worked.

"If you just... Well, I can show you," his father said. "Okay?"

Mike didn't answer.

His father took that as agreement and walked over to the garage. He knelt in front of it, studied it from various angles, and reached for Mike's toolbox.

His steps slow, Mike joined him.

His father explained the problem. "If you've got a couple of two-by-fours, we can nail them in and paint them. Won't be perfect, but it'll keep the critters out."

Mike nodded. He went inside the garage and selected a few pieces from a stack of boards. He held them while his father pounded the nails, and then they painted over them.

While they worked, Mike thought about forgiveness. He wanted to be forgiven by Kayla. His father wanted to be forgiven by him.

They stood back and looked.

"It's better," Mike said grudgingly.

"Why are you doing this if you don't live here?" his father asked.

"My daughter lives here." Mike nodded toward Kayla's house.

"You have a child?" His father's voice squeaked on the last word.

Just then, a pickup pulled up, and Jim Stewart got out. He went to the back of his truck and pulled out a large package. From the image on the front of the box, Mike could see that it was a toy vehicle for Emma, big enough for her to climb inside and drive. There was a big bow on it.

It made sense. Of course Jim, Emma's grandfather, would be invited to her party.

Jim spotted them, put down the box, and walked over. "Looks good," he said, nodding at the garage. He held out a hand to Mike's father. "Jim Stewart," he said.

Mike straightened. "This is my father, Waylon Cook."

"What?" Jim's face reddened and his fists clenched. "When you and your son weren't here for Emma and her mom, I was. And I know what you did."

Mike's father just stood there, listening. No fist clenching from him, and that, more than anything, told Mike that his father had truly changed.

Jim continued to glare at Mike's father. "Whatever goes on between your son and my daughter is one thing, but you...you stay away from my daughter and that little girl." Then he strode off, grabbed the package, and marched toward the house, his back stiff, anger in every movement.

Mike glanced over at his father. To his shock, Mike felt a little sorry for the man, even though he agreed with Jim that his dad needed to stay far, far away from Kayla and Emma.

Mike's father cleared his throat. "We can do better than that," he said, nodding in the direction Jim had gone.

"What do you mean?" Mike asked, puzzled.

"We can get her a bigger gift. I can. Got a little money."

Mike thought of the doll he'd been planning to buy Emma. It was expensive, but small. The box wouldn't be much larger than a shoebox.

He watched Jim make his way into the house, barely able to fit the giant package through the door. His competitive streak rose up.

"It's worth a try," he said. "Let's go."

On the way to the big-box store where Mike and his father hoped to shop for a wonderful gift for Emma, Mike veered off at a local nature trail.

"Mind if we take a walk first?" he asked.

He was really trying to process the fact that he was driving his dad somewhere in a car. The man he'd hated for so many years was right there beside him.

"I'd like that," his dad said. "I appreciate being out in nature, especially since I went so many years without it."

The reference to his years in prison made Mike uncomfortable for reasons he didn't really understand. He only knew that he was glad he didn't see any familiar cars here.

His dad had once been good-looking, but now he was shabby and timeworn. Mike couldn't help thinking of neat, attractive, successful Jim Stewart, Kayla's father. The comparison with his own father was striking.

They got out of the car and headed down a nature trail. Towering pine trees surrounded them, their boughs making a green canopy overhead. Sunlight filtered through the branches, dappling the path where they walked. The sounds of frogs and birds surrounded them. In the distance, he could hear the cry of a hawk. It reminded him of the area where he'd grown up, fifty miles to the southwest.

"I guess you have questions," his father said. "But first, I want you to know, again, how sorry I am for what I did."

Mike waved a hand. He didn't really want to hear his father's apologies.

But his father seemed determined to go on. "I deprived you of a mother and a home, and that was after being no kind of a father to you. I deserve way more punishment than I got for that, and I don't blame you if you never forgive me."

Mike sucked in the rich, fertile air and blew out a breath. "I don't know what to say. I've carried a lot of hostility for a lot of years, but also..." He trailed off.

His father waited with seeming patience, something he'd never had as a younger man.

"I'm afraid I'm like you," Mike blurted out. "That I'll do something like you did."

His father didn't answer, and after a few steps, Mike realized he was walking alone and turned back.

His dad stood still, staring at him. "You? Like me?"

Mike nodded. "The rages. I have them, too."

His father tipped his head to one side and studied him. "Ever hurt anybody?"

"Gave a few kids bloody noses back when I was in school." Mike shook his head ruefully, remembering. "Once I got into football...no. Not outside the playing field."

"Good." His father nodded. "You had some

anger in you, even as a boy, and it was no wonder, given what you were living with. You learned to manage it by now?"

Mike was startled to hear his father say that, startled that his father thought it could be managed.

Then he thought about it more as they walked on, the ground springy with pine needles, moss, and loamy soil. He remembered his conversation with Tyrell, in which he had advised the teenager how to control himself through breathing. Then, with a sense of shame, he thought of his anger at Winston.

But his answer to his father's earlier question still held. He hadn't hit Winston, even though he'd wanted to. "I do manage it pretty well," he said finally. "Not all the time."

"It's a process," his father said.

"You still have issues with anger?" Mike asked sharply.

"I do. But not nearly as often. I got a lot of counseling, and I prayed a lot. With God's help, and with support from the Christian community in prison, I've managed it so far."

"How?" Mike asked. "You used to be way out of control."

His father nodded. "Do you know Second Corinthians, how Paul prayed to have a thorn taken away and it wasn't?"

Mike nodded.

"'My grace is sufficient for you, for my power is made perfect in weakness.' That's Second Corinthians 12, and you should read the whole thing. I do, every day."

Mike was starting to believe in his father's jailhouse conversion. "Is it sufficient?" he asked. "God's grace, I mean? To control your anger?"

His father nodded slowly, looking off toward the horizon. "I believe it is." He looked at peace, like a different person.

Like God had made him a new man.

They walked along quietly for a few more minutes, listening to the waterbirds, smiling together to see a line of turtles on a log, plunking one by one into the water. A squirrel darted up a tree, chattering.

Could Mike actually learn something from his father? Could he forgive him? Should he try?

He didn't have to think hard to remember numerous Bible verses about forgiveness. A couple of sermons, too.

He'd forgiven the minor stuff: Kids who'd teased him in school, women who'd tried to play him for his money, coaches who'd been rough or unfair. He'd even forgiven the guy who'd tackled him and caused his career-ending injury.

But he'd never even tried to forgive his father. That had seemed beyond anything God could want of him.

Now, breathing in the pine-scented air, he revisited his long-held belief that his father's actions were unforgiveable.

Maybe they weren't. Maybe nothing was unforgiveable.

Father, forgive them; for they know not what they do.

If he ever forgave his dad, maybe he could forgive himself, too.

It would definitely be an ongoing process.

They reached the far point of the loop, and the trail turned back. After a few minutes of walking, his father spoke again.

"I pray for you every day. Have for five years, ever since I became a Christian."

"Thanks," Mike said. He felt awkward. He had been a Christian for several years now, too, but he'd never prayed for his father.

"I followed your career, too. Bragged to the guys about you when we watched a game where you played. You were good."

Mike had never considered that his father might watch his games, but of course, they were televised and no doubt shown in prison.

"But," his father went on, "I'm just as proud now that you're a teacher. You're like your mom. She was so smart, read all the time."

A memory flashed in Mike's mind of his mother curled up in a chair, reading avidly to the point where she didn't hear anything going on around her. He'd forgotten that until this moment, but he realized it must've been a way for her to escape her difficult home life.

"She read to you, too," his father went on. "You always liked the biographies about great people."

Another memory came to Mike, then, a visual image of a shelf of thick picture books, red, white, and blue. He had buried himself in them when he was sad or lonely, or when his parents were fighting. The books had piqued his interest in history. They'd given him role models of men and women who'd lived heroic, impactful lives.

His mother must've gotten them for him. It was a ray of light in his childhood, and another thing he'd forgotten until now.

Of course, the books had been left behind on that traumatic night when his mom had died and he'd been swept into foster care. Amidst the chaos, and during his subsequent transfers from home to home, there hadn't been space for a shelf full of books.

Embarrassingly, his throat tightened up, and his eyes felt painful and watery.

They walked on, more slowly now. After a moment, he got control of himself. "Thanks for that," he managed to say. "I'd forgotten, and it's a good memory."

"Your mother was a good woman. She just had a lot of anger, and I brought it out in her. We brought out the worst in each other. And we didn't have faith to help us, nor family and friends, living out in the country the way we did."

He looked over at Mike as they reached the parking lot. "No excuses," he said. "I take the biggest part of the blame for our fighting, and all the blame for what happened...at the end."

There were tears in his eyes, spilling over, but he seemed unashamed. He brushed them off, shaking his head. "You were the best of both of us," he said. "She'd be so proud of you. Like I am. Don't let what we did block you from happiness. Just stay close to the Lord and you'll do fine."

Mike nodded, looking off into the distance where blue sky met the horizon. He wanted to thank his father, but he still couldn't speak.

As they climbed into the truck and headed on their way, Mike felt...different. Like some dark place deep inside him had been blown wide open.

***

The birthday party was over. Kayla flopped back on the couch and rested her head, looking up at the ceiling.

Only Kayla's father, plus Shanae, her husband, Herb, and Maliyah remained. Maliyah and Emma were having a good time playing with Emma's new toys. Emma was most excited about the child-sized car her grandfather had brought, but she'd been persuaded to play with her smaller gifts until the next day, when he could come over and assemble it.

Jim, Shanae, and Herb were chatting about Tumbleweed Days, which took place every Memorial Day weekend.

The party had been exhausting for Kayla, given her stressed-out state of mind, but Emma was so happy. She loved being the center of attention with her friends, and Kayla had prepared gift bags so the other girls wouldn't feel upset while Emma opened her presents.

"Well, sweetheart, this was fun, but we should go on home and get dinner," Shanae said to Kayla. She helped Maliyah put on her jacket and gather her things, and the three of them all headed out the door.

Kayla's father went into the kitchen, and Kayla heard the water running. He was cleaning up the dishes. Really? When had that change happened?

She should go in and help him, and she would, in just a minute.

She reflected on the three years of Emma's life. She'd been so terrified when Emma was born, scared she couldn't manage it alone. But she'd done the right thing coming back to Tumbleweed. Even though her father drove her to sheer frustration sometimes, they were closer than ever. Lately, her dad really seemed to be softening.

Emma came over and leaned against Kayla's legs. "Where's Daddy? Mittens misses Daddy."

"I don't know, honey," Kayla said. She didn't want to lie to her daughter, or make false promises that Daddy would be bringing her a birthday present. She suspected that he would at least send something to Emma. She'd seen him outside earlier, repairing the garage with his players.

She knew the repair job was an apology, a concrete way he could help her. It made her feel a little more charitable toward him. It suggested he wanted to still be involved in Emma's life, which was the main thing. But her hurting heart was glad it also showed that Mike hadn't forgotten about Kayla, not completely.

The doorbell rang. It was probably Shanae, coming back for the covered dish she'd brought and forgotten to take home.

She grabbed the fruit plate and went to the door.

When she opened it, all she saw was a huge blue teddy bear. It was as tall as a large man.

She peeked around and saw that Mike was behind it. She sucked in a breath.

"Is there a birthday girl here?" Mike asked.

"Daddy!" Emma screamed. She ran to the door and shrieked again when she saw the bear. She hugged the bear and hugged Mike, and Kayla grabbed Mittens to keep the little cat from escaping.

"Come on in," she said. What else could she say? Her feelings about him were mixed, but she was so glad he'd come to see Emma on her birthday.

He set the bear down on the couch, and Emma cuddled up to it, climbed into its lap, and tugged at the ribbon around its neck.

"Now, where am I going to put that?" Kayla asked Mike. She tried to inject annoyance into her tone, but she couldn't conceal the fact that she was happy he'd brought it. Happy that he seemed overcome with emotion, his eyes shiny.

Jim came out from the kitchen, wiping his hands. "A little big, isn't it?" he said.

"Not much bigger than the car you got her," Mike said.

Jim glared at him.

Mike glared back, then his face broke into a smile.

Jim held out for a moment and then smiled back.

Kayla's phone dinged, and she pulled it out of her pocket to see a text from Shanae.

"There's a man outside your house. Thought you should know."

Kayla went to the picture window and looked out. A tall, rough-looking, gray-haired man stood on the sidewalk, looking up at their house. He looked just slightly familiar. She looked over at Mike and then back at the man. "Who is that man standing outside?" she asked.

Mike extricated himself from Emma and the bear. He came over to the window. "That's my father," he said. "He helped me shop for Emma's gift. Paid for most of it."

Kayla looked at the man again as what she knew about him flashed through her mind.

Jim came up behind them. "No way. He's not coming in."

"You're right, he's not coming in," Mike said. "He knows that, but he was hoping to catch a glimpse of Emma. I told him to head on out, that I'd send him a picture of her with her bear, but I guess he didn't go."

Emma, always curious, dragged her bear over to them, climbed up on the back of the sofa, and looked out. "Who's that?" she asked.

"Someone Daddy knows," Kayla said. "He helped Daddy get your bear."

Emma nodded, accepting the explanation. She pulled her bear up beside her and made it wave at Mike's father.

The man froze, his hand going to his mouth.

Kayla's throat tightened. Mike's father hadn't been a good man, hadn't lived a good life. But he was Emma's grandfather, and apparently, that meant something to him.

The man outside waved back and then walked slowly down the street.

Kayla had so many questions, but she didn't want to ask them in front of Emma and her father. Besides, Emma's eyes were starting to droop. It was time to feed her something resembling a healthy snack and then let her relax with a couple of picture books. Kayla had a feeling Emma would fall asleep quickly tonight.

Mike touched Kayla's shoulder. "Would you consider taking a walk with me?"

She tilted her head, looking up at him. "Maybe. Why?"

"There are things we need to talk about," he said.

"Sure, I guess."

"I can give this little lady a snack and watch some TV with her," Jim said. "Give you two a chance to talk."

Kayla looked at him, surprised. She wouldn't have expected him to be an ally of Mike. Apparently, she was wrong.

Maybe she'd been wrong about a few things.

They pulled on jackets against the evening chill and headed out into the twilight. Soon, they were strolling toward town. A few people were out in their yards, and some cars drove by, but for the most part, the evening was quiet.

She stole a glance at Mike. He was looking into the distance, frowning. So handsome that he made her heart hurt, but that wasn't all she felt.

Knowing what Mike's father had done, realizing that Mike had forgiven the man enough that they could shop for Emma's birthday gift together, gave her pause. Could she ever be that forgiving? Could she ever open her heart to a person who'd done such a terrible wrong?

Could she forgive Mike?

She'd been judging him harshly ever since he'd come to Tumbleweed. Ever since Emma's conception, truth be told. She'd blamed him for getting her into the difficult situation of becoming a mother unexpectedly. She'd blamed him more for leaving her to raise their daughter alone.

The truth was, she was equally responsible. She could have worked harder to contact him, but she'd let her own hurt feelings rule her, even though she now saw that having Mike in their lives was the best thing for Emma.

She'd definitely judged him for backing away after they'd kissed. But the reality of seeing his father, seeing the pain on Mike's face as he'd looked out at the man while Emma had waved to him, had humbled her. Mike's life had been hard. Of course it had impacted him in many ways, inside and outside.

She had felt sorry for herself all these years for having an overbearing father, had thought herself virtuous for forgiving her dad. She'd resented the illness that had taken her mother from her too young.

But her own problems paled in comparison to the horror Mike had faced at a far younger age.

"So," Mike began, and she looked over at him. His troubled expression hurt her heart.

She touched his arm. "You wanted to talk about something?"

"I do." Mike cleared his throat. "Kayla, I've been so wrong about so many things. I've hurt you badly, and I'm sorry for that."

She shook her head. "I understand. You've been through a lot."

His eyes widened. "No, you've been through a lot. You've raised our daughter alone. You've been amazing and open to me throughout this whole bizarre month. You're a wonderful mother—the best."

His words were a balm to the scared, insecure part of her. She had never felt completely confident as a mother, and she hadn't been sure she was doing the right thing letting Mike in. "Thank you for saying that," she said quietly. "It means so much to me."

"There's a lot more I need to say. First thing is, I want to stay and be a father to Emma." His forehead wrinkled and there was concern in his eyes.

"That makes me really happy because it will make Emma so happy," she said. "I want you to stay and be involved in her life. It's the best thing for her."

He smiled, but a muscle jumped in his jaw. "There's more," he said gruffly. "Kayla, I… I want to be a partner to you."

She stopped and studied him, tilting her head to one side. "A partner? What kind of partner?"

He took her hand and guided her to a bench in front of the beauty shop.

Just before she turned and sat down, she saw that Ariella's sister, Ginger, was sweeping up and pretending not to look at them.

She didn't care. She just sat beside Mike and looked up at him.

"Not just a partner in parenting," Mike said. "I want more than that. And more than friendship, too. I want to be a real partner to you."

She stared at him. "You do?"

He took a deep breath and smiled at her, a little tentatively. "You're such a good person. When I see you, you're all I think about. I'm wild about you—so much it scares me. But I'm learning that I don't have to be so possessive, that I can control my anger. I'll keep working on it, probably forever. And I was wondering..."

Kayla could hardly stay seated, could hardly breathe.

He squeezed her hand. "Would you consider dating me?"

She sucked in a breath, staring at him as the truth in her heart revealed itself to her. He was everything she wanted and hadn't believed she could have. He was handsome and fun and smart. Even better, he could admit that he was wrong and could speak emotionally. He was a blessing, and her gratitude nearly overwhelmed her.

She wrapped her arms around him, ignoring the fact that inside the beauty shop, Ginger was openly staring at them.

"I would love to date you, Mike Cook," she said. "When can we start?"

Epilogue

The next Sunday after church, the usual community luncheon was outdoors.

It was a beautiful, springlike day, with a soft breeze and warm sunlight. Trays of barbecue, coleslaw, and macaroni and cheese sat on tables, filling the air with tantalizing fragrances.

Kayla walked past it all, pausing when she saw that there were several pecan pies on the dessert table. Dad would be thrilled that his favorite dessert was so well represented. In fact... Kayla had to wonder whether several of the church ladies knew of Jim's preference and had baked a pie, hoping he'd notice them. Was her father starting to be thought of as an eligible bachelor among the single church ladies?

The thought made her smile. Everything made her smile. It was a good day, the best day. Because she and Mike had an understanding. They were going to try to make this thing between them work and grow.

Mike had come over early this morning to spend time with Emma, and it had been wonderful. Emma was delighted to have her daddy there to help cook breakfast. When Emma was busy playing with Mittens, and Kayla was washing dishes, Mike had come up behind her, and they'd shared a kiss.

But Kayla had sensed a reticence in Mike. A couple of comments he made suggested that he doubted she would stick with him. That, given who his father was, he was a lowlife and destined to stay that way forever.

His insecurity made Kayla's heart ache, partly because she understood it so well. There was a part of her that didn't quite believe in their relationship, either.

So Kayla had made a decision.

Across the group, standing beside the shelter house where picnic tables were laid with food, Kayla spotted her father in deep conversation with Mike. Her father, unsurprisingly, was doing most of the talking. Mike was nodding and smiling, but there was, again, a little bit of that reserve in Mike. She didn't like to see it.

She headed over and put an arm around both of them. "What are you two talking about?" she asked.

"Just like I told him," her father said, "that

lawsuit is a thing of the past. Winston Compton will be going to military school next year."

Kayla softly clapped her hands together. "I know we're supposed to like all of our students," she said, "but Winston has been a troublemaker for as long as I've known him. The school will certainly be more peaceful without him."

Mike said, "The idea is that he may be able to play football there. I wish him well."

He spoke with sincerity, and Kayla's heart warmed. He was such a good man. "Playing football in a new place would be good for him," she said.

"It would," Mike said. "Football is a great way to get out those aggressions. I should know."

Kayla's father clapped Mike on the back. "You're doing a fine job with our boys," he said. "Now, where is my granddaughter?"

Kayla gestured toward the field that adjoined the picnic pavilion. Emma was running around with Police Chief Daniel Montgomery's four-year-old twin nieces, under the chief's watchful eye. "Chief Montgomery is so sweet to babysit his nieces while his sister and her husband are away for the weekend," she said. "Emma is thrilled to play with them."

"Maybe," Mike said, "the police chief is here

to keep an eye on my dad." He clearly meant the words to be a joke, but to Kayla's ears, it sounded forced.

Mike's father had attended church today and was here at the luncheon, too, sitting on a bench with a couple of older people. Waylon was watching Emma with a poignant expression on his face.

Kayla and Mike had agreed that it would be better for Mike's dad not to get to know Emma or speak with her just now. He was leaving for an oil rig job next week. If he kept himself clean and stayed out of trouble with the law, then they would reconsider letting him become part of Emma's life.

Church secretary Hannah Bryant came over with a tray of cookies and offered them to Mike's father and the others sitting beside him, stopping to chat in her friendly way.

Pastor Rob waved as he crossed in front of them, moving toward a group of women who were calling him over.

"Now, he's a good guy," Jim Stewart said.

"He's been a big help to me," Mike said.

Kayla knew that Pastor Rob had been counseling Mike informally for the past couple of weeks. It was yet another great thing about Mike: He was open to receiving help. "He seemed lonely," she said. "Is it true that he's only here for a year?"

"That's right," Jim Stewart said, "and the year's halfway over. We all hope he stays."

"Hope who stays?" Patty Wright came over, greeted Kayla and Mike with a "Hi, Sweetie" and a hug for each of them, and then stood beside Jim. The two of them shared a glance that seemed to Kayla to be a little more intense than just friends. Was her suspicion correct? Were the two of them starting to have some feelings for each other?

"Did you manage to get Ben to come along?" Jim asked her.

"I did," Patty said. "Bit of a struggle, but his kids and I talked him into it."

Patty's son, Ben, was a single dad who was usually busy with his ranch, the Big W. Maybe it was grief over the loss of his wife that had made him grouchy, or at least aloof. If anyone could pull him out of it, though, it was Patty.

Jim and Patty drifted off, leaving Mike and Kayla standing alone together. He started to put an arm around her and then pulled it back. So she hadn't been imagining it. He was reserved around her. Maybe he didn't like public displays of affection, and that was fine, but she sensed something deeper. "Let's go sit on the bench over there," she suggested.

"Sounds good to me." He did put his arm around her as they walked over to a bench on the edge of the field where Emma was playing. Butterflies fluttered above flowering grasses, and the air smelled fresh.

Kayla's heart was pounding. She took Mike's hand in both of hers. "I want to ask you something," she said.

"Anything." He was smiling at her, that gorgeous smile that always lit her up.

She sucked in a breath and exhaled. *You decided to do this, now do it.* "Will you marry me?"

"What?" His mouth fell open, and then he tilted his head and shook it, as if he needed to fix his hearing. "Did you just ask me...to marry you?"

Now that the biggest hurdle was out of the way, her words tumbled over each other. She squeezed his hand. "I don't want to wait," she said. "Mike, you're a wonderful man. You've come out of a very tough background and situation, and you're stronger for it. You're so kind—to your students, to Emma, and to me. Everyone in this community loves you and... I do, too."

He was staring at her as if he wanted to devour her words. But he didn't speak.

Was she wrong about this? Was he regretting his suggestion that they date?

Push forward. Do it. "I have to know," she said. "I have to know if you mean it this time. I have to know you won't run away."

He looked at her for a long moment, with deep feeling communicated in his gaze. "Oh, Kayla, I love you so much," he said as he pulled her into his arms and held her tight. "I would be completely honored to marry you."

She cried with joy as she melted into his arms.

Apparently, public displays of affection weren't a problem for him after all.

But they *were* in public, with church friends not that far away and most likely watching them. She pulled back a little and glanced around. Yes, a small crowd had gathered and were watching them openly.

Mike touched her cheek, and she turned back to look at the man she loved. To her surprise, he was grinning. "Great minds think alike," he said. He reached into his pocket and pulled out a small box. Then he sank to his knees. "The truth is, I drove to Beaumont last night after we talked. Caught the jewelry store right before it closed, and called Shanae for a guess about your ring size. I figured I'd find the right time to ask you, eventually. But like in so many things, you're way ahead of me." He held out a beautiful, square-cut diamond ring.

She gasped and sank to her knees in front of him, and he steadied her and held her close. "Put it on," he urged her, and she slid the ring onto her finger. It fit perfectly.

"Mommy! Daddy!" Emma rushed to them and joined their hug, nearly knocking them over.

There was applause from the crowd in the picnic shelter.

Kayla lifted her face to the sunshine as she relished the embrace of her daughter and the man she loved.

God had blessed her beyond anything she deserved. He'd forgiven her mistakes and brought her to this joyous moment.

"I love you both, so much," she murmured. And she thanked God for the bright hope He'd given her, and for the future ahead of them.

* * * * *

Dear Reader,

Thank you for joining me in Tumbleweed, Texas! It's been so much fun to write this book, not only because I love the characters, but because I got to collaborate with three other authors to bring this series to life. Tina Radcliffe, Mindy Obenhaus, and Jill Kemerer are a dream to work with, and I know you'll love their upcoming books in the Tumbleweed series.

Kayla and Mike both have significant challenges to overcome. Kayla has been raising a child alone and trying to build an identity for herself apart from her wealthy family. Mike's past left him feeling like damaged goods. Both of them need faith and a supportive community to reach their full potential and help their daughter grow up feeling strong, healthy, and loved. Fortunately, Tumbleweed is just the place for that!

I didn't grow up as a football fan, but living in the sports-oriented city of Pittsburgh, I've learned to love the excitement around the game. It was a lot of fun to create a hero who'd been a part of that world. I did grow up in a family of educators: my grandparents and my mother were teachers, I taught for thirty years, and my sister and daughter both currently teach, too.

It was a joy to portray Mike and Kayla as educators who truly care about students and help them to thrive.

I'd love to have you subscribe to my newsletter, where you'll find giveaways, updates on coming books, and photos of my mischievous pets! And please come back to Tumbleweed next month for the next book in the series, *The Pastor's Easter Prayer*, featuring Pastor Rob and church secretary Hannah Bryant.

Happy reading,
Lee

Get up to 4 Free Books!

We'll send you 2 free books from each series you try PLUS a free Mystery Gift.

FREE Value Over $25

Both the **Love Inspired®** and **Love Inspired® Suspense** series feature compelling novels filled with inspirational romance, faith, forgiveness and hope.

YES! Please send me 2 FREE novels from the Love Inspired or Love Inspired Suspense series and my FREE gift (gift is worth about $10 retail). After receiving them, if I don't wish to receive any more books, I can return the shipping statement marked "cancel." If I don't cancel, I will receive 6 brand-new Love Inspired Larger-Print books or Love Inspired Suspense Larger-Print books every month and be billed just $7.19 each in the U.S. or $7.99 each in Canada. That is a savings of 20% off the cover price. It's quite a bargain! Shipping and handling is just 50¢ per book in the U.S. and $1.25 per book in Canada.* I understand that accepting the 2 free books and gift places me under no obligation to buy anything. I can always return a shipment and cancel at any time by calling the number below. The free books and gift are mine to keep no matter what I decide.

Choose one:
- ☐ **Love Inspired Larger-Print** (122/322 BPA G36Y)
- ☐ **Love Inspired Suspense Larger-Print** (107/307 BPA G36Y)
- ☐ **Or Try Both!** (122/322 & 107/307 BPA G36Z)

Name (please print)

Address   Apt. #

City   State/Province   Zip/Postal Code

Email: Please check this box ☐ if you would like to receive newsletters and promotional emails from Harlequin Enterprises ULC and its affiliates. You can unsubscribe anytime.

Mail to the Harlequin Reader Service:
IN U.S.A.: P.O. Box 1341, Buffalo, NY 14240-8531
IN CANADA: P.O. Box 603, Fort Erie, Ontario L2A 5X3

Want to explore our other series or interested in ebooks? Visit www.ReaderService.com or call 1-800-873-8635.

---

*Terms and prices subject to change without notice. Prices do not include sales taxes, which will be charged (if applicable) based on your state or country of residence. Canadian residents will be charged applicable taxes. Offer not valid in Quebec. This offer is limited to one order per household. Books received may not be as shown. Not valid for current subscribers to the Love Inspired or Love Inspired Suspense series. All orders subject to approval. Credit or debit balances in a customer's account(s) may be offset by any other outstanding balance owed by or to the customer. Please allow 4 to 6 weeks for delivery. Offer available while quantities last.

Your Privacy—Your information is being collected by Harlequin Enterprises ULC, operating as Harlequin Reader Service. For a complete summary of the information we collect, how we use this information and to whom it is disclosed, please visit our privacy notice located at https://corporate.harlequin.com/privacy-notice. Notice to California Residents – Under California law, you have specific rights to control and access your data. For more information on these rights and how to exercise them, visit https://corporate.harlequin.com/california-privacy. For additional information for residents of other U.S. states that provide their residents with certain rights with respect to personal data, visit https://corporate.harlequin.com/other-state-residents-privacy-rights/.

LIRLIS25